DUPLICITY

THE HARRY STARKE NOVELS
BOOK 23

BLAIR HOWARD

For Jo
As always

1

THE LATE-NIGHT KNOCK ON HER DOOR DIDN'T COME AS A surprise to Isabella Rossi. Having sons who were involved in New York City's underworld came with a price, and at that moment, the late-night visitor was the least of her worries. In fact, she was hoping they might, by some rare chance, be of some help.

She limped to the front of the house, the arthritis in her knee acting up again. She'd never been a fan of living in the Bay Ridge area of Brooklyn, and when she'd moved into the small house on Shore Drive, she told herself it would be temporary… But that was almost twenty years ago now, and the only thing that had changed was the ever-increasing rent.

One day, I'll make it back to Staten Island, she thought.

Pushing the longing thoughts aside, Isabella peered through the peephole, and recognizing the face, she turned the knob and pulled the heavy door open a little.

"Why're you here?" she asked, peeking out, looking around to make sure he'd brought no one with him.

"I'm here 'cause you said you wanted to talk, Izzy." His voice was rough, much like the rest of him. He couldn't have

DUPLICITY

been a day over twenty-five, but Izzy wasn't sure he had even that many years under his belt. His tussled dark hair hung damply around his face, the waves framing his high cheekbones and penetrating brown eyes. He was of Italian descent—she knew that—but she wasn't sure which family he was connected to.

Not that she cared. "You got anyone with you?" she snapped.

"Nope." He popped the *p* on the word. "You gonna make me stand out here in the rain, or what?"

She pursed her lips, stepped to the side, and nodded for him to come in. "You got anything for me? The number he left me didn't have no names with it. So I'm assuming that's why you're here, right?"

The young man sighed. "Yeah, and like I told you, maybe it's better that we just let him be. If he ain't around, it's probably for good reason."

"He's my *son*," Isabella replied, narrowing her eyes. "And when we talked on the phone, you promised you were gonna help me find him. He's got a kid. He's got a girlfriend. He didn't just decide to take a vacation." Frustration laced her words, but there was also a sadness with them as well. She didn't want to raise her grandson without him. She'd already done that with her own boys.

"Look, Izzy, I'm not saying I'm not going to help you find him." He pulled out one of the chairs at the small table in the space just off the kitchen. It wasn't big enough to call a dining room, but it was something, and that small table had been packed with friends and family many times.

Izzy raked her fingers through her thick, dark hair and then pulled out a chair across from him. "There has to be something you can tell me. *Please.* I know Matty didn't just disappear into thin air. Somebody did something to him, I know it."

"You don't know it," he snapped back at her. "You don't know nothin' about him, Izzy. All you know is the cute little Matty that came to you for family dinners and holidays. I *know* the real Matty, and if something happened to him... well, I don't know that I wanna go poking my nose in it. I don't got a death wish."

"I'm not..." She trailed off. *Was* she asking him to put his life on the line to locate her son? *Maybe.* Maybe she was, and maybe that was asking too much. "I'll go start digging and knocking on doors myself if I have to."

"No." He was fast to stop her, holding up a hand. "No, you don't wanna do that. You'd be walking into a den of vipers, Izzy. You're gonna have to trust me."

"I don't trust anyone, *Lake.*" She used his nickname because that was the *only* name she had for him. Neither he nor Matty had ever offered anything other than *Lake.*

"Good, you shouldn't." He leaned toward her, his dark eyes intense, giving her an unsettled feeling. "And for the record, Izzy, I don't trust no one either; not even Matty."

Anger nipped at her. "I don't know what you're trying to say, but you better not badmouth my son in *my* house."

He chuckled, the sardonic sound filling the small house. "You don't know what you're getting into, Izzy. And the truth is, I don't think he wants you poking around."

"You say that like you've talked to him," Izzy snapped, her anger now tempered with a glimmer of hope. "If... if he's just hiding out 'cause he's in some trouble, just tell me. I won't keep searching for him. I'll call off the hounds."

Lake's thin lips turned downward. "Izzy... I really wish I could tell you I knew something, but I don't. I don't know where he went—or why—but I know he wouldn't have taken off if he didn't have a good reason. Matty Junior's his entire world. He ain't gonna leave his kid. Or Catherine. Or you."

DUPLICITY

She wanted to believe him, but the changes she'd seen in Matty lately made her second guess his loyalty to his family. He'd become paranoid and had acted strange, missing dinners and panicking if the blinds were left open. Something had been amiss, and before she could ask him what it was, he'd disappeared into thin air. At first, she thought maybe it was drugs, but everyone swore he was clean...

The silence hung heavy in the room as Isabella pondered the next step. She wanted to go to the police, but she was worried about the consequences it could have if she did. Matty's life was complicated, and the last thing she wanted to do was put a target on his back.

"I'm looking for him," Lake said quietly. "I swear, I am, Izzy. I don't know where he's at, and ain't *no one* talking right now."

Her heart fluttered. She sucked in a ragged breath. "It's bad, isn't it? Just tell me the truth. Do you think I'm gonna have to bury my son before his thirtieth birthday?"

Lake was quiet for what seemed like an eternity, then said, "I don't know. Like I said, I don't have any answers right now. I came to see you because I know that's what Matty would've wanted me to do. I hope you don't gotta bury him. That would mean I'd have to bury him, too, but..."

"But this is the way it is, working for the families," Isabella said softly, so softly she wasn't sure if Lake even heard her. "I hate it. I wanted better for my sons."

"We all want better for ourselves," Lake said, his expression growing distant as he stared over her head, his eyes fixed on the old clock. "I still tell myself sometimes that *this* isn't it for me, that there has to be something more. But..." He paused, locked eyes with her, then continued, "I don't think I'll ever get out of this city. And if I do, my guess is it's gonna be in a body bag."

"Don't say that," Isabella scolded him, her voice heavy with emotion. "You all got so much life left, and all you have to do is choose to walk away and start over."

Lake laughed, shaking his head. "Right, and you know what happens when one of us tries to pull something like that? We end up in pieces at the bottom of the bay, Izzy."

Her heart sank at the thought of Matty ending up like that—maybe he already had. "I just need to know where my son is," she said, "and you know I'm not too timid to knock on the doors myself."

Lake's face contorted with concern. "You *can't* do that. Matty wouldn't want you to, either. It's gonna get ya killed. Then, who's Matty supposed to come home to, huh? Catherine? We both know they ain't gonna make it. Catherine doesn't give a rat's ass about Matty."

"Yes, she does." Isabella couldn't help but argue. She and her son's girlfriend had their differences, sure, but she thought Catherine was reacting the way any woman would whose significant other was involved in... Well, *seedy* business endeavors was putting it mildly. "She's taking care of Matty Junior all on her own, you know."

"Yeah, okay," Lake muttered, pushing himself back from the table. "I told ya, and I'll tell ya again, I'm doing the best I can. Don't go knocking on no doors, and don't go to the police. I'm working on it, and I'll keep working on it. I won't let you go down, too. He wouldn't want that."

Isabella nodded, choosing not to get up from the worn-out table. She'd told herself that she'd get a new one many times, but now, she wasn't intending on ever getting rid of it. Matty had sat at that table the last time Isabella had seen him, and she hoped that, like some sort of lucky charm, it would bring him back to it.

"I gotta get moving," Lake said, his voice gruff. It grated on her nerves to listen to him speak like that. He was always the quiet one of the two, and now he was the only one. "I'll let you know when I know something, but don't expect any answers to come quick."

"I won't, but…" She looked up at him. "At some point, I'm gonna go to the cops, Lake. I won't sit around and wait for someone else to do my job as a mother."

His eyes darkened. "Then may God keep you safe. The more you poke the bear, Izzy, the more likely it is to strike back."

2

FINN DOYLE

I never expected the Irish mobster to show up in my office, nor did I particularly want him there. I wanted to put Morrigan Doyle and her Ponzi scheme far behind me. It had been one hell of a case, and I had no intention of getting involved any further with her family.

"Look, Harry, I don't expect ya to loik me," Finn grunted, placing his large hands on his knees.

I'm not usually one to pay attention to someone's hands, but this man's were larger than most and covered in long, jagged scars.

I don't even want to know what caused those, I thought.

"I'm not taking any new cases right now," I said, which was the truth. I rarely offered my services to anyone unless they were Kate Gazzara. Most of the time, the people who came to us seeking help came by referral, and then we were picky about the ones we took.

But it was more than that. I did *not* want to get involved with another Doyle.

"Ah, but see, now, dis is different," Finn said earnestly in his thick Irish accent, digging into the pocket of his leather jacket. "Dis is something personal to me." He pulled out a worn leather wallet and then fished out a picture. "This is my *friend*, Matteo Rossi."

I watched the crinkled photograph as he slid it across my desk. I scrutinized the young man in the photo. There was nothing about him that was out of the ordinary. He had dark chocolate-colored hair and matching eyes. A light shading of facial hair graced a square jaw, and though the picture was only from his shoulders up, I could tell by the thick neck he was a brute of a man. Probably a gym rat, and he had the look of Italian descent about him.

"He's a good friend of mine," Doyle continued, "and he's been missing for nearly a month." He tapped the picture. I looked up at him. "I just want to find him and make sure he's okay. He's got a family, so he has. His kid needs him, Harry."

I pursed my lips, waiting on my gut feeling to tell me one thing or the other, but it stayed quiet. Finn *appeared* to be genuine, but there were plenty of people who *appeared* to be a lot of things they were not. And so I decided to give him a chance. "Lay it out for me, Mr. Doyle."

The man's face brightened. "All right then. So I will. Well, y'see, his girlfriend, Catherine, she said he didn't come home a month ago today, so, uh, July twenty-seventh would be the date."

I nodded, grabbing a pen and notepad and scribbling down the date. Even though I wasn't planning to take the case, especially as it was an obviously iffy missing person case. I also make a point to write down information I don't need versus *not* writing down something I might need later. Sounds a bit convoluted, doesn't it? But I'm sure you get the idea.

"He didn't show up for a meeting we had planned last Friday, either," Finn continued, leaning back and folding his arms across his chest. "And that's not like him. He *always* shows up. He's a punctual kind of guy. And that's when I really began to worry."

"You don't think he just needed a break? People do that, you know?" It was a counter card everyone in law enforcement had said many times, and it was something every person who reported a missing person—other than a young child—had heard.

The irritation showed on Finn Doyle's face. "I *think* you'd be the kind of investigator that didn't play off a man's worry wantin' to search for his friend."

"What about his family?" I ignored the jab. "Why hasn't his family reported him missing?"

Finn's upper lip twitched. "Because maybe they don't have the funds to fly to Chattanooga to speak with a private investigator that may or may not even take the case. Not everyone has such wealth at their fingertips."

I narrowed my eyes at his cheeky response. "The local police would've been a good choice. Or they could've called me or found an investigator in New York."

"That gets nothing accomplished, and you know it, Mr. Starke," Finn shot back at me, his green eyes bright. "The police see him as a grown adult. They're not interested. So, I took the time to fly down here to meet with *you*. It wasn't some simple endeavor, either. And don't you underestimate me, sir. I'm willing to beg for your services if I have to." The man was clearly easily agitated, and I harbored my amusement internally.

"I'm listening to you, Mr. Doyle," I responded patiently. "I'm simply stating the obvious. What else do you have for me? Other than the picture, of course."

Finn Doyle relaxed, albeit subtly. "Well, that's the problem. I don't have much of anything. It seems as though he just vanished into thin air. He even left his cell phone and wallet at his girlfriend's place."

"Odd," I muttered. "Anything else?"

"I don't have the wherewithal or the capabilities to hunt him down the way you might think. Sure, we have our connections, but they're not nearly as extensive as yours. I do have a couple of addresses, though. That's the best I can do."

I didn't believe a word of it, but I kept that to myself. "I would have thought your *organization* would've been able to come up with *something*," I said, leaning back in my chair and folding my arms.

"Do I have to repeat m'self?" His upper lip twitched again. "I *can't* find him. It's truly as though the man dissipated into thin air. He's frickin' vanished, so he has, and Oi'm concerned."

I took a deep breath, looked again at the photo and said, "Is your *friend* involved in the same business as you?"

Finn shifted in his seat, narrowed his eyes, pursed his lips, then said, "He... Well, yes, he *is*." He paused for a moment as if to gauge my reaction; I didn't give him one. "He's involved in *my* organization, and before you put two and two together, *yes*, he is Italian. He's an odd man out, which is why I'm so worried about him."

"Ah, I see." *I don't need to get involved in this mess,* I thought, but for some reason, I still felt compelled to dig. "Did he have enemies, anyone who would want to hurt him?" I had the feeling it would be a long list, but it was a question that needed to be asked. And I was pretty sure the answer depended on where Matteo Rossi fell on the Irish mob's pay scale.

"Now, you're not going to believe this, Mr. Starke, but I don't really know." Finn Doyle's shoulders dropped. "He was just a low-level employee. Not a man predisposed to startin' a foight, if y'get me meanin'—though he wouldn't be averse to finishin' 'em if he had to. He was a talker. That's for sure, but I can't think of anyone that he truly pissed off."

"But you have rivals," I said. "So, assuming he really is missing and has not just taken off somewhere, could it be business-related?"

Finn shook his head. "I don't think so. We've not had any issues with our Italian rivals for quoit a while. We have our territory; they have theirs. Matteo didn't get involved in any of the higher-up stuff. Knocking him off wouldn't have accomplished anything."

"Maybe it was done to get at you?" I reasoned. "As you said, he is your friend."

"I don't think so." He seemed certain, his tone firm and demanding. "I don't know what happened, or why, but I want to find him. And besides, when a rival takes out one of your men, it's always a power move, or it's done to get your attention. That doesn't happen when someone just disappears. When that happens, it's usually to make a statement. The body may not show up, but *something* always does."

I nodded, hating the idea of wading into the gray territory of the mafia, Irish or Italian. "I'll have to talk this over with my partner. I don't believe it's something she'll want to take on... or me, for that matter."

"Foine." His voice was sharper now. "But turning me down would be a mistake."

Of course, it would. You might come for me in my sleep, and it wouldn't be the first time. I pushed back from my desk and stood up, ignoring the comment. Being threatened after decades in law enforcement was nothing new. Ninety-nine-point-nine percent of the time, the threats were empty; the rest of the time, I survived.

"I'll speak with Jacque and then get back to you," I said

with a smile. I didn't play into his attempts at intimidation. To me, it was just another day at the office.

"If you'll give me a moment—"

I left my office and went to find Jacque.

"You want to take on a missing mobster?" I asked, peeking my head through the open doorway.

Jacque looked up from her computer, her brows raised. "So that's what Mr. Doyle wanted, huh? Strange request."

"He says the guy's a friend, and he thinks something bad's happened to him."

"Wouldn't be surprising given the line of work he's in," Jacque said, straightening up in her chair. "In fact, if something *did* happen to him and they don't want us to find out, it could be hell to pay for us."

"Ah, now, don't act like we haven't encountered adversity before," I teased, smiling at her. "It's more of a headache than a danger, I think. The guy went missing in New York City. Quite a way from home. Not to mention, Jade's still getting over a stomach bug."

She nodded. "Seems like you have your answer, then. No!"

I gave her another nod and then turned to go back to my office, only to find the mobster standing right behind me.

Great. He's an eavesdropper, too. I did not know how long he'd been standing there.

"Look, I heard ya, and I'm beggin' ya," he said, his hands together as if praying. "Will you just look into it? And keep an open mind. I gotta have an answer for Catherine."

I looked back at Jacque. She shrugged.

I heaved a breath and gave him a wry look. "I could... I suppose, *look into it.* And by that, I mean simply to decide if we'll take the case. No promises."

Finn lowered his hands. "Okay. I'll take that."

Good, because that's all I'm offering.

3

"So, that's it, huh?" Jacque joked after I had seen Finn out of the office. "All the man had to do was beg a little, and you caved. Just like that."

I rolled my eyes at her. "All I said is that we'd look into it and decide based on our findings. You know I'm just going to put Tim on it. Have him gather some financials, phone records, background checks and, you know, the usual. It'll be enough to give us an idea of what's going on."

"Why even bother?" Jacque gave me one of her looks. "What you went through with Morrigan Doyle was, to say the least, exhausting. Never mind the danger."

"Well, yes," I said. "But that was then, and this is now. As far as I can tell, it's just another missing person case. And the perceived danger has never stopped us from taking a case. You know that, Jacque. It's part of the job."

"And part of the job is also bein' mindful of getting ourselves into situations that we'd be better off stayin' out of." Her curt response and lapse into her native Jamaican accent were surprising, as Jacque tended to be more adventurous and, typically, up for a challenge. But then again, she was right; the Morrigan Doyle case had been more than I'd bargained for.

And aren't most of the cases we take on? I thought.

"I'll have Tim run the basics," I said, "and then we'll move on, okay? That should appease our Irish mobster... Though he did say we might regret *not* taking the case, or something along those lines."

"Oh, that's just great," Jacque huffed. "He's already makin' threats, and we haven't even begun to look into it yet."

I grinned at her. "I don't know. I kind of like the excitement."

She rolled her eyes at me. I smiled and winked at her, then turned away and headed along the corridor to Tim's cave, leaving her grumbling to herself.

Tim's cave, as we like to call it, is one of a kind and the IT hacker's dream. Technology isn't my forte, but I was fairly certain there was nothing that Tim couldn't track down. Now, putting the squirrelly fella out in the field? I wouldn't ever recommended it.

I rapped twice on the door and then turned the handle. I pushed it open and squinted into the dimly lit interior. I don't know why the man wants to keep the lights off, but it's his domain, and therein, he's the boss.

"Hey, Harry," Tim greeted me, turning in his chair to look up at me over his dark-rimmed glasses.

"Those new?" I gestured to the glasses.

"What?" He looked confused. "These?" He pushed them further up the bridge of his nose with a forefinger. "Yeah." He grinned. "I got 'em yesterday."

"Very nice," I said. "How's the new server working for you?" We'd just done a major upgrade of his equipment.

"Fine, I guess..." He paused. "No, it's better than that, boss. Thank you."

I nodded as I stared at the double bank of monitors that formed a quarter semicircle around his station.

"Good," I said, "because I have a new task for you."

He raised his eyebrows as I handed him the photo of Matteo Rossi that Doyle had provided. "Just a picture? That all you got?"

"And these," I said, handing over the list of names and addresses. "The guy's missing. He was last seen on July twenty-seventh, so I'm told. Though, how reliable the source is... well, you get the idea."

Tim nodded as he scanned the list of addresses. "They're all in New York City?"

I nodded. "They are."

"Okay..." he said, and for a moment, I thought he was going to question me, but he didn't. "I'll see what I can find."

"Matteo Rossi is his name. I don't have the middle name."

"Shouldn't need it for me to find him." Tim laid the list and photo down beside his primary keyboard. "What're we looking for?"

"Well, he's missing, so... financial records, credit cards, cell phone records, anything that might indicate he's still among the living. Do a full workup."

"Okay... yeah, gotcha. I can do that. Shouldn't take me long. I'd say by tomorrow, I should have something for you."

"Good," I said, "but you need to be aware he has ties to the Irish mob."

He scrunched up his nose, did that thing with his glasses, squinted at me, then said, "Rossi, huh?"

"Yeah, I know. Italian man, Irish mob. I guess they're into DEI these days," I joked, then chuckled, but Tim didn't. He just stared at the information with a perplexed expression on his face.

"You don't think they... because he's... you know, *Italian*."

I exhaled with a sigh and shook my head. "I don't know what you're trying to say, Tim, but if you're asking if he could be the victim of a hate crime, your guess is as good as mine. For all we know, Matteo just up and moved to California."

"Right." Tim laughed. "I'll see what I can figure out and get back to you."

"Thanks." I gave him a pat on the shoulder and let him get to work, leaving him there in the semidarkness. Me? I didn't intend to spend any more time thinking about Finn Doyle.

Once seated at my desk, I sifted through some of the ongoing cases while considering hunting down the relevant members of my team for updates. However, I decided to wait, finishing up some of my own clerical work instead. Being a private investigator means juggling more than one case at a time, so it's a lot of organizational time.

I wonder how Jade is feeling.

The thought crossed my mind as I exited out of my email. I took my cell phone from my pocket and pulled up Amanda's number, hitting the call button, and waited. We'd given Maria time off while my wife stayed home with our sick daughter, hoping Amanda wouldn't catch the bug.

"Hey, honey," Amanda answered, her voice groggy, as if she'd been sleeping. "How's work?"

"How about, how're you and Jade?" I countered, smiling to myself. "It sounds like you've been napping."

"You'd be correct." She sighed. "Jade's still asleep. Being up all night did her in, I think. She needs the extra rest."

"Sounds like you do, too."

"Oh, yes. Don't think I haven't thought about taking a quick siesta when the lights are low and the house is quiet."

I chuckled, happy that she still had a sense of humor. Amanda's one of the strongest women I know, and she's been through the wringer in the past, confronting much more dangerous situations than a preschooler with a stomach bug. If anyone could handle it, it was her.

"You think you'll be home in time for dinner?" she asked, yawning as she spoke.

"Yes," I replied. "It's a nothing kind of day. D'you need me to pick anything up on the way?"

"No, we have everything we need here." As she said the words, I heard our daughter's voice muffled through the phone. "Uh-oh, Jade is up. I'll see you when you get home. Love you."

"Love you both," I replied with a smile, my daughter's whiny tone bringing an even bigger grin to my face. My family had become the most important part of my life, though to the outside world, one might think I was still putting the job first.

I set my phone down on the desk and then got back to the tedious paperwork. Finn Doyle's missing person case stayed at the front of my mind, however, and, for some reason, I found myself unable to shake it, and that bothered me. The last thing I needed was for my mind to run away with a situation we more than likely were not going to pursue.

That being said, the rest of the day went by in a bit of a blur, but I welcomed it. As I stood up from my desk at five that afternoon, I stretched to work out the kinks of six or more hours of sitting and decided I'd need to go for a run that evening. So, I gathered up my laptop and headed for the door, only to find Jacque outside, hand up as if she was about to knock.

"Well, that's good timing," I said with a chuckle. "I take it you were coming to check on me?"

She raised her eyebrows. "Oh yeah, I was just checkin' to see if you'd maybe died from boredom." Her Jamaican accent—she switched it on and off at will—only enhanced the playful scowl.

"Ah, is that what it was, then?"

She shook her head. "No, I thought I'd walk you out."

This time, I was the one who made a face. "Walk me out? I'm not decrepit or—"

"It has more to do with the black Tahoe sitting out front in the parking lot, right next to your Range Rover." She sounded concerned.

I nodded. "Good call, Jacque," I said. "Let's go see who's waiting on me." And I led the way out, conscious of the heavy weight of my CZ75 in its holster under my left arm. "Has Tim found anything?"

"I don't know," she replied. "He's been squirreled away in his cave all day. Heather and TJ have already left. I think they're curious, though. TJ mentioned it. They know when Tim gets in the zone, he's usually into something interesting."

I nodded, opened the door to the lobby and stood back to let her through.

"I don't know if it's interesting or not, but I hear what you're saying. I really don't want to get us involved with the Irish mob again, but there's something niggling away at the pit of my stomach that tells me something about Finn Doyle is not quite right. Let's hope Tim finds nothing and we can forget about it."

We stepped out into the open, and Jacque locked the door.

"Relax, Harry." Jacque laughed as we headed across the parking lot. "Let's see who your watcher is."

As we approached the SUV, the driver's side window rolled slowly down. My hand twitched. I was prepared for the worst. Paranoia? Perhaps, but understandable after the events of the past several years. This time, however, it was uncalled for.

"Have ya made up yur moind yet?" Finn Doyle asked, his eyes darting back and forth between Jacque and me. "Seems loike yuh had all day."

"It's not that simple," I said coolly. "It takes time—"

"It shouldn't take ya that long to decide whether or not you're gonna take me case," he cut me off, his voice chilly. "I'll only be in town for a short while, so I will, and I need an answer. Otherwise, I'll have to find someone else."

And I wouldn't argue with that.

"How long will you be in town?" Jacque asked before I could say anything.

"A couple a days," Finn said, continuing to glare at me while answering her. "That's it."

Jacque nodded. "We'll have an answer for you by then. Have a good evening, Mr. Doyle."

Finn let out a sharp huff and then rolled up his window and started the engine. The Tahoe's tires squealed as he reversed and then whipped out of the parking lot, leaving us standing there, watching.

"Excessive," Jacque muttered, shaking her head.

"Man's a lit fuse," I added.

We said our goodbyes and parted ways. I climbed into my car, started the engine, put the selector into drive and headed toward Broad Street and Lookout Mountain. *I'll need to keep an eye out for Mr. Doyle,* I thought. *I have a feeling he's not going to be easily put off.*

4
───────

I HALF EXPECTED FINN DOYLE TO FOLLOW ME HOME THAT evening, but he didn't.

I pulled into the garage some twenty minutes later, feeling just a little uneasy. And the feeling lasted until I walked into the house to the sound of Jade's giggles.

Ah, she must be feeling better, I thought as I stepped into the dining room, where my dark-haired, bright-eyed preschooler was sitting at the table with a plate of spaghetti in front of her. Amanda, seated to her right, was watching her carefully.

"I can't imagine that being good for a sick stomach," I said as I leaned over and planted a kiss on the top of Jade's head.

"It's what she asked for," Amanda said as she looked wearily up at me.

"My tummy doesn't hurt anymore," Jade told me, a giddy grin on her face. "I feel all better now."

I smiled at her. "Well, I'm happy to hear that." I pulled out a chair and sat down beside Amanda.

"Are you feeling okay?" I asked. "You're not eating."

She gave me a weak smile. "I think… so," she replied. "I

think maybe it's just, you know, environmental. My stomach isn't quite up to the idea of spaghetti right now."

I nodded. "Why don't you go rest for a while? I'll get Jade settled for the evening... Look, I need to pick your brain later about... Well, about a potential case."

Her expression brightened. "Oh? That sounds exciting, and yes, why don't you do that? I'm desperate for a shower. I must look awful."

I smiled at her. Shower or not, she looked beautiful even with her hair pulled up and wearing an old pair of gray sweatpants and a T-shirt, but I wasn't going to argue with her.

"Go ahead," I said, thinking I'd postpone my run until after Jade was in bed. It being late August, it would still be light until late, not that I didn't enjoy pounding the pavement in the dark. I did. In fact, I found it quite relaxing.

It was after seven-thirty when I finally got Jade into bed. I'd taken my time enjoying a somewhat stilted conversation with my one and only child. She rambled on and on about something called the Magic Roundabout that Amanda was streaming for her. Chattering on about Florence and Dougal and... Briar the *snail?* I shook my head, smiling.

I tucked her into bed, kissed her on the forehead, and stepped away. I stopped at the doorway, turned and smiled, knowing it wouldn't be long before she'd be a teenager, *and what will the world hold for her then?* I wondered.

"I know what you're thinking," Amanda said as she joined me. "Stop it. She'll be fine."

"How do you do that?" I asked. "How d'you know what I'm thinking?"

"I don't," she replied, "but I do know *you*. Now go on I'll say goodnight to Jade and join you in a minute."

I changed into my running gear, then went down to the kitchen where Amanda was already waiting for me.

"So, you're going for a run?" she said. "I thought you wanted to talk." Amanda sat down at the breakfast table, cradling a glass of pinot noir in her hands.

"Yes, I am, and I do. Talk first, run later. No harm in being prepared," I said, grinning at her. I chuckled, pulled out a chair and sat down. "You're not going to like this," I began. "Finn Doyle came to see me today."

"Finn Doyle?" she said, sitting up straight. "As in related to Morrigan Doyle?"

"The very one," I replied. "Finn is her son. He wants me to find his friend. I don't think we should take it on. The problem is, it's made a place for itself in my brain."

"Oh, that's never good." Amanda laughed softly.

"You're telling me."

"So… it's another missing person case?" she said.

I nodded. "That's about the size of it."

"Who's the missing person?" she asked.

"As I said, Finn showed up at the office today. Apparently, his friend, Matteo Rossi, is missing and has been for a month. I initially turned him down, but I have Tim running some checks just to see where it goes."

Amanda took a deep breath. "The Irish mob?"

I nodded. "Yes, and I know where you're going with this. Rossi is Italian, but I don't know if that matters much these days. But it might. Who knows? Rossi has a family though, but that's not it. I have one of those feelings. If I decide to take it, I'll have to travel to New York City again."

Her shoulders slumped ever so slightly. I'm sure she didn't realize she'd visualized her concerns.

"Morrigan Doyle could be involved," she said. "Maybe it's a ruse to draw you in and…" She trailed off, knowing I knew what she was thinking.

I shrugged. "Could be," I admitted. I hadn't thought of that.

"I don't think it is, though. If she was trying to entrap me, I would have thought she'd use something she *knew* I couldn't resist. This one I can."

"True." Amanda took a sip of her wine, looked at me over the rim of the glass, and then said, "I just find it a little... *odd.* It will mean a lot of travel, Harry."

"That's also true," I said, "but they do have ties to Chattanooga," I reasoned. "That being said, I really don't know what I'm going to do. My brain's telling me not to take the case. My gut's telling me the opposite. Who knows what kind of rivalry it might involve? And I've just about had my fill of the mafia, for now."

"For now," Amanda echoed and then laughed. "Oh Harry, that's so you."

I grinned at her and then stood up. "I know, I know, but for now, I'd rather steer clear."

"I like the idea of that," Amanda joked, then stood up, stepped around the table, grabbed my hand, pulled me to her, wrapped her arms around my neck and kissed me. Then she pulled away, let out a long breath, and said, "Harry. Do what you have to do. It's who you are."

I looked into her eyes and nodded. "What about you? Are you going to work tomorrow?"

She nodded. "I told them I'd be back in the office tomorrow."

"Well then, why don't you relax; take it easy? I'll see you when I get back."

"Be careful out there, big boy." Amanda poked me in the chest. "You never know who might be lurking in the shadows."

"Geez," I said. "Thank you for that." I kissed her forehead and slipped out the front door, eyeing my surroundings. The sun had sunk behind the mountain, casting an unearthly purple glow where the sky touched the earth. The slight breeze, the fresh air and the warmth made for a glorious evening. I love to run. I run in all kinds of weather. On a night like that one, though, it's pure delight and just what I needed to clear my head.

I took off along East Brow Road, heading south, my earbuds hanging loose around my neck. Most times when I run, I use only one earbud, but for some reason, I left both out. Why? I didn't know. Maybe it was simply a need to enjoy the quiet sounds of the night and the stunning views from the mountaintop. Maybe it was my gut telling me something. I'd learned a long time ago never to ignore my gut. It saved my life more times than I can remember.

And so, I ran at a good clip, my tennis shoes pounding the pavement, my eyes fixed straight ahead. Our home on Lookout Mountain is just outside the Chattanooga city limits but still only twenty minutes or so from downtown. I didn't think Finn Doyle would bother me up there on the mountain, but who knew? There was no telling what he might do.

I will not be pressured into taking the case, though, I thought as a bead of sweat ran down my cheek. I've never been one to be pressured into doing anything. I take only the cases that I think I can solve, and let's face it, when someone with mafia connections goes missing, the end is usually predictable, and it's not good.

I made the turn at the three-and-a-half-mile point, breathing easily, and headed back toward the house. By then, it was fully dark. The sky was clear, and the stars were bright. The constellation of Orion was overhead and a little to the south. It was quiet; the stillness of the night seemed almost palpable.

I turned left onto West Brow and slowed my pace a little. And then, just as my house came into view, I saw a pair of headlights in the distance. I slowed my pace almost to a walk, watching them as they grew closer. I continued on, warily. But then, the vehicle—a dark SUV—made a hard right, completed a U-turn and headed back the way it came. I was either watching someone who'd made a wrong turn or... someone was watching me.

5

I WOKE EARLY THE FOLLOWING MORNING WITH A FEELING I couldn't shake, though how to define that feeling, I wasn't sure. My stomach felt uneasy, that I do know. Amanda was already up and about, so I showered, dressed, and went downstairs to the kitchen to be greeted by the smell of fresh coffee.

"Daddy!" Jade yelled, waving at me.

"Good morning, sweetie," I said and kissed the top of her head.

"Coffee?" Amanda said, placing the cup on the table.

"Thanks," I said, grabbing it up. "You slept well." I said it as a statement rather than a question.

"No, I didn't," she replied, "and neither did you. You tossed and turned all night."

"I did?" I said, frowning, then took a sip of my coffee. "I can't think why," I lied.

I could see Amanda was about to make a snippy reply when Maria walked through the door, a big smile on her face.

"Good to see you," I greeted her, thankful for the diversion. "Jade's back to her normal self."

"I am happy to hear that," she said and pulled out a chair beside my daughter. "All better, huh, baby?"

Jade grinned. "Uh-huh, and I'm ready to play."

Maria laughed, reaching out and squeezing her shoulder.

Maria Pérez, a tall, dark-haired, attractive fifty-two-year-old, was our nanny, but not just any nanny. An ex-ATF officer, she was as handy with a Glock as she was with a diaper. I hired her more as a bodyguard than a nanny back in the day when Shady Tree was an ever-present threat to me and my family. Shady is gone now, but Maria remains. She loves Jade as much as we do and is a superb cook, too. What a bargain she turned out to be.

We made small talk for a few more minutes before I said it was time for me to leave. So, we said our goodbyes and then went our separate ways.

I was running a little behind when I made it into Chattanooga that morning, and skipping breakfast hadn't helped the queasy feeling in my stomach. So I swung through Subway and grabbed a six-inch steak, egg, and cheese on flatbread. I pulled into the office parking lot where, much to my delight, Finn Doyle was nowhere in sight.

I parked in my reserved spot and wolfed down what was left of my sandwich before heading inside, where I was surprised to find most of my team waiting for me in the reception area.

I eyed Jacque with my eyebrows raised in question, then glanced at Heather, TJ, and Tim, who had dark circles under his eyes. My guess was he'd been there all night, which wasn't unusual.

"Before anyone starts anything," I said, "let me make myself some coffee, and then we'll meet in the conference room in, say… five minutes." I eyed them warily as I passed through, ignoring their looks. They all seemed to be a little on edge, and I had to wonder why.

I went to the break room and filled my mug, noting the

muffled voices outside. It wasn't often something like that happened—that my team became so invested in something—and again, I had to wonder why. I stood for a moment, sipping the bitter liquid, wondering what the hell was going on. Was it the Doyle case? I needed to find out.

I walked into the conference room, took my seat at the head of the table and said, "All right, what's this all about?"

It was Tim who answered.

"Matteo Rossi," he said, holding up the small photo that Finn Doyle had given me. "This is him."

"Okay..." I drew it out, wondering if Tim's lack of sleep was catching up to him. "And?"

"And... I can't find him. I can't find anything. Nothing, other than a social security number and a New York driver's license."

"Oh, come on, Tim," I said a little impatiently. "There has to be something. No one is invisible these days."

"He's *not* invisible," Tim agreed. "I can confirm that this man in the picture is Matteo Rossi. However, that's only because of this." He turned his laptop around so I could see it. I found myself looking at a Facebook page.

Find Matty Rossi. I read the headline and saw a photo of the same man in the photo Doyle had left with me. The photo on the screen showed a grinning dark-headed man cradling a baby.

"This is all I have."

I shook my head. "That's impossible."

"I thought so, too," Tim muttered, clearly fatigued by a long night at the keyboard. "But someone has attempted to erase Matteo Rossi out of existence."

"Interesting," I said as Tim turned the computer back again and began flipping through the screens.

"He's not listed at any of these addresses, and when I went

deeper, I realized that his information had been deleted—permanently—by a cyber company called Del-Opt."

I glanced around at everyone. Heather shrugged and shook her head. TJ looked stoically back at me, his arms folded across his chest. No one spoke.

"I've never heard of them," I said.

"I've used them," TJ said, his voice a soft growl.

TJ is the man everyone wants on their team, because *no one* wants him on the opposing team.

Kate Gazzara brought him to me. She found him homeless and about to cash in his chips, but then he discovered the body of a young woman in a back alley. Kate was the investigating officer, and she saw something in him that nobody else did, so she brought him to me. It turned out he's a decorated Vietnam vet—a Silver Star and two Purple Hearts. He did two tours. The first in 1968. The second 1972. He was a Marine turned accountant, the victim of a shady bank officer who accused him of stealing from the bank where he worked to cover his own crimes. TJ was innocent, but he was convicted and did some time. It ruined him. Ronnie Hall, my white-collar crimes investigator, had just quit and I needed a replacement, so I hired TJ, and I've never regretted it.

He's saved my butt on several occasions and is, at seventy-one, way older than the rest of my team, but he's also in better shape than any of them, including me. This is because of the rigorous workout regimen he embarked upon the day Jacque took him in hand. TJ is six feet tall, slim and weighs one hundred ninety pounds. He wears his white hair closely cropped. He keeps his heavily lined, deeply tanned face cleanly shaven. TJ is also a killer, as I've found out… twice.

"They just remove your information from public access online, is all," TJ said matter-of-factly.

"Okay, so now what?" I asked no one in particular.

Tim sat up, poked his glasses and nodded. "But that's just the beginning. Matteo Rossi has been removed from all the public access sites, but even that shouldn't have stopped me from finding non-public information."

"Continue," I told him and took another sip of my coffee.

"He doesn't have a bank account, no cell phone records, no credit card information, no police record that I can find. I even—and you're not going to like this, Harry—I even tapped into the state data banks, the IRS and..." He took a deep breath. "AFIS and NCIC, and other than just his birth certificate, I'm at a loss."

"What about aliases?" I asked.

Tim shook his head. "Everything I can find on him is pre-adulthood."

"How old is he?" Jacque asked.

"He'll be thirty in two months, according to the birth certificate," Tim answered, flipping over to it. "His father died twelve years ago, widowing his mother. He's got a brother, Micah. That's all I got."

"Were you able to track either of them?"

"Yes," Tim said, pulling up the Facebook page again. "This is his mother, Isabella Rossi. His brother, Micah Rossi, is four years younger than him. He's got a record—and a lot of arrests."

"But Matteo doesn't?"

Tim shook his head. "No, as far as I can tell, he's clean."

"Hmm" was all I could come up with to say. It didn't make a lot of sense for Matteo to have a squeaky-clean record, especially with him being involved with the Irish mob.

"No one wiped that, I don't think," Tim said quickly. "The guy just has a clean record. There's really no way for someone to truly hide that from me. But I'm surprised the guy doesn't even have a cell phone?"

"Burner," Heather spoke from behind us. "It's not that

uncommon. If he was involved in something dicey, he could've easily chosen to use a burner."

"And paid for everything in cash," Jacque added. "It would be a huge pain, but maybe that's how he chose to live his life. It's not unheard of."

"Very difficult to accomplish, though," TJ said. "Is there a chance he just closed the accounts down? I mean, he could've closed them if he wanted to disappear."

Tim shook his head. "He had a minor account with his mother prior to turning eighteen, and that was closed years ago. Since then, there's been nothing. I mean, I've searched, really searched."

I took a deep breath, inwardly processing the information. There had to be an explanation. "Maybe he uses a fake identity."

Tim rubbed his eyes. "I searched through anyone associated with him or his family. I can't find any connection. I have to admit…" His cheeks reddened. "I'm stumped."

"So, all we have is that?" I motioned to the Facebook page still up.

"I'm… I'm afraid so." Tim frowned, glancing down at it. "His mother has a Facebook page, and that wasn't too hard to find. I can run a trace on her easily enough, same with the brother. They're not living in the shadows. Her address is the same as the one you gave me. It makes no sense that Matteo is… for all intents and purposes, a ghost."

I nodded. "We need to get in touch with Isabella. But I find it a little strange that they created the Facebook page, but they're not working with Doyle to find him."

"Well, I see that Finn Doyle is a close family friend." Tim scrolled to another page, which I realized was the mother's. I stood up, rounded the table and leaned over to see an image of Finn with his arm draped around Micah Rossi's shoulders.

"Where's Matteo in this picture?" I asked, searching the faces of the dozen or so people surrounding a birthday cake on a table.

"I don't know," Tim's voice dropped again. "He's not in any of the pictures."

"What the hell?" I mumbled, shaking my head. "Why?"

"I can't answer that," Tim said and straightened up in his seat. "It's weird."

"Maybe he's not who he says he is," TJ said. "It smacks of witness protection to me. Maybe he's a nark."

I nodded. "Witness protection?" I thought aloud. "That makes sense. Maybe the feds scooped him up and got him out of there."

"It's a reach," Heather said. "But I guess *maybe*. I don't know why they'd try to get rid of his identity, though. That seems like a lot of unnecessary work, even for the feds."

"How many pictures is Finn Doyle in?" I changed the subject back to the Irish mobster. "Just the one?"

"No," Tim answered, pulling up a file. "He seems to be closely involved with the family. In fact, he was there at the birth of Matthew Rossi, who is Matteo's young son. There's a picture of Finn holding the baby."

"But there's only *one* photo of Matteo holding the baby," I said. "Which is the one posted on the missing person's page, right?"

"Right." Tim sighed. "And that's where I'm hung up. I was able to find the mother of the child as well; her name is Catherine. Her social media is private, but I was able to hack into it. She hasn't posted anything in years."

"Maybe the guy just likes his privacy," Heather said. "After all, not everyone trusts the internet. Me included. I don't have much of a footprint either."

"But you have a bank account," I countered, scratching my

chin. "That's where I'm at a loss. There's something more to this Rossi fella."

"I say we take the case," TJ spoke up. "I'm curious. I want to know who the hell this guy is."

I looked across the table at him, smiled and shook my head just as the bell chimed for the front door.

"I'll go see who's there." Jacque gave me a look and said, "I'll be right back."

"I don't know, TJ," I said skeptically. "If we take this on, we might all end up in New York City—"

Before I could finish the thought, Jacque stuck her head in and said, "Finn Doyle is here, and he wants an answer. Now."

6

"I don't think we should take it," I said, falling in step with Jacque. "I have a feeling it could explode into something we don't want to deal with."

"The team seems to be invested," she replied.

I shook my head. "I don't like it. We'd have to travel to New York City ASAP."

"At least it wouldn't bring danger to our own door," Jacque reasoned, stopping me before we reached the reception area, where I assumed Finn was waiting for us. "I say we ask a large retainer, and then if he's willing to pay, we take the case. Make it worth our time, with no promise that we'll find the guy. It's been a brick wall so far. And, who knows, maybe Doyle will spill more information if we accept the case. Go talk to him."

I heaved a sigh and shook my head. "So we're taking the case," I muttered as I stepped through the door into the reception area. Finn Doyle rose from his seat, smoothing out his tie. He was wearing a suit, a stark contrast to the black T-shirt and jeans he was wearing the previous day. I smiled to myself, thinking, *Maybe he thinks I'll take him more seriously.*

"Good morning, Mr. Starke." He stuck out his hand. "I'm

sorry if I'm comin' across as a little pushy, but I have to know if you're going to take me case. If not, I have a meeting with another detective."

One that must have a dress code, I thought to myself. "Let's chat in my office."

"All right," he answered and turned to pick up his briefcase.

I glanced at it, wondering about the contents.

He saw me looking at it.

"Nuttin' sinister." He grinned. "I can open it for ya, if you like me to. I'm hopin' what I have in it'll bribe ya to take the case."

I resisted the urge to shake my head.

"If you'll follow me," I said and led him through to my office.

I unlocked the door and stepped inside for the first time that day, noting that the air smelled a little musty.

I flipped on the light and went to the chair behind my desk, gesturing for him to take a seat in front.

"Well?" Doyle asked, setting the briefcase down beside his chair. "I need to know, Mr. Starke."

I didn't appreciate the pressure but chose to ignore it.

"I've decided to take the case," I said, the words bitter in my mouth. "But I'm going to need a retainer, one hundred thousand dollars. It's going to require a lot of travel, and, as I'm sure you already know, Matteo Rossi is not an easy man to find."

Finn's lip twitched. "I suppose…" He paused, straightened his tie, and then, to my surprise, continued, "Good enough, Mr. Starke."

He reached for the briefcase, set it on his knee, flipped the catches, popped it open and set it down on my desktop. I looked at it. It was full of cash. *Terrific. Maybe I should've asked for more.*

"Dere's one-hundred-fifty grand in dere." Finn said. "You can take your time countin' it."

I eyed the cash and then pushed the case to one side.

I nodded and said, "I'll take your word for it, Mr. Doyle—"

"Now, why don't ya call me Finn?" he said, cutting me off. "After all, we're partners now, are we not?"

And that really pissed me off, but I played along. There was no point in antagonizing the man from the get-go.

"Very well, Finn it is, so let's get down to business, shall we?" I asked, taking a notebook from my desk drawer. "What can you tell me about Isabella Rossi, Micah Rossi, and the mother of Matteo's child, Catherine? You're close to the family, as I understand it... What's Catherine's last name, by the way?"

Finn's smirk disappeared. He looked disgruntled. "It's McCarthy, and yes, I was very close to the family for much of me life. Matteo and me, we grew up together. But then Isabella blamed me for getting Matteo involved in me... Well, me family business. Once he went missing, she pushed me out. She t'inks that it's all my fault, but like I told ya, I don't know anythin' about what's happened to him, and I've made me rounds, trust me."

I didn't trust him, but I *did* believe that he'd been looking for him. The mob like to keep such things to themselves. Bringing me in was probably an act of last resort.

"And you found nothing?" I said.

"Not a damn t'ing," Finn replied quietly. "It's like he dropped off the map. There's no trail to follow."

"D'you think something could have happened to him?" I asked.

"You mean do I think he's dead?" he replied. "I don't know. I hope to hell he isn't, but that's for you to find out, now isn't it?"

"Let's assume he's still alive," I said, ignoring the question.

"Why would he want to disappear? Is he in trouble... with your people or... his own?"

"I don't know why he'd want to run," he said. "He isn't in trouble with my people, as you put it. The Italians..." He shrugged. "I don't think so, but who knows? Matteo is a private person, so he is. He doesn't like people to know his business."

"Any aliases?"

Finn was quiet for a moment, appearing to mull the question over. "I don't think... I don't think so. Look, Mr. Starke, Matteo's just a low-level..." He paused, obviously thinking how to put it. "He hadn't worked his way up," he said, eventually, "and I don't think he wanted to. He liked to get his hands dirty, if you know what I mean. He's a scrapper, so he is, and like many such as he, he couldn't give up the thrill of the fight."

I didn't like where this was going. "So, he was an enforcer, a hitman? Is that what you're trying to tell me?"

Finn shook his head and laughed. "No. I wouldn't exactly call him that. He was... Let's call him a handyman, a man you call on to slink around in the dark and do the things that might get ya dead."

"And that's probably what happened to him," I said, once again reverting to my original theory.

"No," Finn snapped. "I told ya, Mr. Starke, I'd know if something like that happened to him. I'd know it, for sure. Things like that don't get covered up; they're an example."

There was a knock on the door. Jacque stepped in and shut the door behind her.

"I've brought the paperwork for Mr. Doyle to sign," she said, dumping a stack of papers in front of him. "We need your signature and a check for the retainer before we continue forward, Mr. Doyle."

"Of course." Finn nodded to her. "There's a hundred and fifty grand in dere." He gestured toward the briefcase.

Jacque looked at me, her eyes wide, obviously startled.

Finn looked again at me and said, "If I were you, I'd start with Isabella Rossi and Micah. They're the closest to him."

"What about Catherine McCarthy, his girlfriend?"

"Her, too," Finn confirmed. "She might be helpful."

"Thanks." I nodded, thinking I'd have Tim do a deep dive into McCarthy's background. "If you'll go with Jacque, she'll have you complete the paperwork."

I closed the briefcase and pushed it across the desk to him.

He stood up, nodded, grabbed it, looked at me and said, "We'll stay in touch, then?"

I nodded. "That we will, Finn. That we will."

Jacque picked up the papers and led Finn Doyle out of my office, leaving me to ponder what to do next. We would have to travel to New York. I could have conducted the interviews over the phone, but you can't beat the face-to-face, eyeball-to-eyeball interrogation. Body language is… well, it's a language all its own, and you can't read that over the phone.

And when it came to Finn Doyle… well, I still hadn't made up my mind about him. He was willing to pay a lot of money to find his friend, but I couldn't help but wonder how genuine he was. Was he really just a worried friend? Or was he up to something more sinister?

Then again, he was close to the family, I thought as I tore the sheet of paper from the notepad. That fact played into the investigation. He could've been acting on behalf of the family, or maybe even trying to right himself with them.

I had no answers and no theories.

I sighed, shook my head, pursed my lips and stood up, then paused for a moment staring down at my desktop, thinking. But my mind was blank, white space. I gave it up and went to the conference room, where I assumed everyone would still be talking things over. I was right.

"Catherine McCarthy," I said, handing the sheet of paper to Tim. "The girlfriend. See what you can find out about her."

He nodded, took the paper from me, and I sat down.

"I take it you took the case, then?" Heather said.

I took a deep breath and said, "I did! I'm still not sure it was a good idea, but it's done, so let's get started. We need to decide when—and *who*—is going to New York. I have a strong feeling Finn isn't going to let up until we have the logistics figured."

"I'll go," Heather offered with a shrug. "I could use a trip out of town."

"I think you should go, Harry," TJ spoke up. "You and Kate went the last time. You might encounter some familiar faces."

"I agree... Geez, Amanda's going to love that." I chuckled wryly, shaking my head. I had no idea what she'd think about me going back to the city and the people that brought so much danger, but it looked like that's where I was heading.

7

FORTUNATELY, FINN DOYLE DIDN'T HANG AROUND LONG AFTER completing the paperwork and taking care of the retainer. Which kind of surprised me. I was also relieved that he'd decided to spend his time elsewhere.

It was late that afternoon and we still hadn't decided who was going to New York. And I still had to speak with Amanda about it, even though I knew she'd be supportive.

She was at work, but I called her anyway.

"Hey," she answered brightly.

"Hi. Look, I'm sorry to bother you at work, but I have some news," I said, getting straight to the point.

"Let me guess," she said. "You've taken the case and you're going to New York."

I frowned. "How'd you know?"

"Oh, Harry," she said and laughed. "Sometimes you forget how well I know you. Any time you come home to talk about a case, it usually means you're going to take it, even when you say you're not. It's what you do."

I sighed. "Well, I might take off sooner rather than later.

DUPLICITY

Heather's going with me, and I think I'm going to talk TJ into going too. I don't know what we're getting into. Last time, we got more than we bargained for."

"Good idea," she replied. She paused, then continued, "You do what you have to, Harry. We'll be fine. I have Maria now that Jade is feeling better."

"Hopefully, it won't take too long."

"Oh yeah?" she said skeptically. "You know how long missing person cases can take. I'll expect you when I see you."

"It shouldn't take longer than a week or so," I said, grabbing my jacket and slinging it over my arm. "I wouldn't go, but I prefer to conduct my interviews in person... You wouldn't believe it," I said, changing the subject. "This guy we're looking for has *no* digital footprint, not even a bank account."

"Sounds like he's an off-grid kind of guy," Amanda commented. "That's not that uncommon anymore."

"But in New York City?" I said. "How can that be? Maybe if he was out in the boonies, but not in New York. No way."

"You're probably right," Amanda agreed. "But he could distrust the government. I've heard of crazier things. You know what happened back in the Depression days? People pulled their money out of the banks."

"Maybe." I paused and then glanced down at my watch. "Why don't I pick us up pizza for dinner? I have to speak with Heather and TJ before I leave, so I'll be maybe an hour."

"That would be fine. Are you leaving for New York tomorrow?"

I hesitated. "I'm not sure. I need to fix getting the jet with August. But yes, I think so. I'd like to get it done and over as quickly as possible, and I have a feeling Finn Doyle won't stop pushing until we do."

"Well, work out the details and let me know," Amanda said. "I'll see you at home. Love you."

"Love you, too," I said, thinking of other things.

I hung up the phone and went to look for Heather. I'd liked to have taken TJ along with me, but on second thought, I didn't like the idea of leaving Jacque here by herself—well, with Tim —but he wasn't much when it came to the crunch. And we still had other cases to work.

I found Heather in her office, frowning over Isabella and Micah Rossi's information. I figured she must have found something that piqued her interest.

"Anything interesting?" I asked.

She looked up and said, "Oh, hi. No, not really. It's all fairly straightforward. The Rossi family is what you'd call upper middle class. Isabella has been at the same address since 1988. Her son Micah seems to be an anomaly, though; a drifter with a record." She handed me the printouts. "See."

I set my things down on a chair and took them from her. "It's all petty stuff," I said. "The guy likes to fight."

"Yeah, he's in the Brooklyn House of Detention awaiting trial for another assault and battery charge." Heather frowned. "I don't understand why this guy has a rap sheet and a footprint, but his brother Matteo is the complete opposite."

"Well, let's hope that when we get to New York tomorrow, someone will provide us with some clarity. Don't worry too much about it right now." I handed back the printouts. "We can go over these on the flight."

"So we're leaving tomorrow, huh?" Heather took the information from me and set it back down. "What time are you thinking?"

"I'll have to call my father and see what I can work out. We'll meet up here first thing in the morning, though," I said. "I don't think there's any need to leave too early. I'd like to give Tim time to ensure he's found us all he can."

Heather nodded. "Sounds good to me. I'll pack and bring everything along with me to work in the morning."

"I'll text you the flight and hotel information as soon as I have it," I said. "I'm calling it a day. I told Amanda I'd pick up pizza, and I have to call August."

We all said our goodbyes, and I headed out, giving TJ and Jacque a wave as I made my way out.

I slid into the driver's seat and started the engine. Then I took out my phone and ordered a couple of three-cheese specialty pizzas and an order of breadsticks.

I chuckled to myself as I hung up the phone and pulled out of the lot, heading to Broad Street and the pizzeria, figuring it would take about fifteen minutes to get there. And then I called my father, August.

"Hey, Siri, call August Starke."

I waited for it to connect, listening to it ring a few times. Finally, just when I thought it was going to go to voicemail, he picked up.

"Hello, son," he greeted me, his voice bright. "How the hell are you?"

I tapped on the steering wheel. "Pretty damn good," I said, matching his gruff approach. "How about you?"

"Same," he said. "So, to what do I owe the honor of this call?" He always was one to get right to the point.

"Well, I have to fly to New York... tomorrow, and I was hoping—"

"Not again," he said with a chuckle. "What is it this time? The last case you had up there got a little dicey, as I recall."

"Well, yeah," I agreed. "But it doesn't seem to matter where I go these days. Dicey is par for the course."

"And no one handles it better than you. You want to use the Gulfstream, I suppose. It's currently in Miami. When do you want to leave?"

"Well, I was hoping to leave sometime tomorrow, if we could make that work. I'd prefer to get to New York before the day is over. We may or may not try to get a jump on the interviews," I said as I pulled into the pizzeria parking lot.

"I think we could make that work. Let me look and see what I can do. I'll send you a text once I have the details figured out. How's that sound?"

"Sounds like a plan," I said, putting the car in park and turning off the engine.

"Now look, son," he said. "This dangerous stuff you keep taking on has got to stop. You're not getting any younger, and you have a family to think of. You hear me?"

"I do, and I agree," I said. "I'll try to do better. Now I have to go. The pizza will get cold."

"Harrumph!" he replied and hung up the phone.

I grinned to myself and stepped out of the car, thinking he was right and that maybe it was time I hung up the gloves and retired. I sure as hell didn't need the money.

I headed inside, greeting the young woman at the counter with a smile, and said, "Order for Harry Starke."

"Got it," she said, nodding. She turned around and grabbed the boxes, then turned again, holding them out to me.

"Thank you," I said. "Have a good evening."

"You, too, Mr. Starke."

It was at moments like those I felt almost entirely normal… almost! As if I wasn't being hounded by mobsters or followed home by shady characters. But I couldn't forget that my wife had been abducted by a serial killer several years ago, or that she'd almost died when one of Shady Tree's henchmen ran her off the road on Lookout Mountain, or that I'd been on the run in Mexico for killing a Texas Ranger, or that I'd just accepted over one-hundred-thousand dollars to hunt down a man for Finn Doyle. It was a pleasant feeling to do something typically ordinary, like picking up a pizza on my way home. But you know, I also knew if I *didn't* have that kind of excitement in my life, I'd be bored out of my brains.

Tonight, though, I was going to relish the normalcy, because tomorrow, we'd be wheels up. And there was no telling what awaited us in the big city.

8

I spent that evening in late August with Amanda and Jade, refusing to think about anything that had to do with Matteo Rossi, other than passing along the information to Heather that we'd be wheels up at eleven the following morning.

We put Jade to bed at eight and then Amanda helped me pack. That done, we spent the rest of the evening just being... ordinary.

I rose early the following morning, had coffee and breakfast with Amanda and Jade, then kissed my girls goodbye, greeted Maria at the door, and headed to the garage.

The morning air was warm but not yet dampened by heavy humidity as it so often was. I stowed my suitcase in the backseat and climbed into the car. Part of me was eager to get to the office, and the other part still questioning why the hell I'd taken the case.

It was a little after eight when I pulled into the parking lot, and the weight of it being the last normal morning I might experience for at least a couple of weeks hung heavy on my shoulders. Usually, such things never bother me, but that day they did.

I slid out of the car, double-checking that no one was hanging around. There wasn't. And so I made my way inside, wondering if Tim had found anything more.

Jacque saw me first. "Morning. Everyone is in the conference room sifting through the information Tim found last night," Jacque said as I walked through the door. "And, Harry." She locked eyes with me. "I think it's best if TJ and I were on standby for this one. If it goes anything like the last Doyle case, you might need us."

I nodded, wishing I had grabbed a coffee. "Good idea," I said. "I agree."

"And… I was thinking about this case last night," Jacque said, eyeing me warily. "What if Matteo is missing for another reason? We know he could've left of his own accord, but what if it's more than that?"

"Like the witness protection idea, you mean?" I asked.

"Well, no," she drew out the vowel sound. "What if he's running from something? I mean, a man who stays off the grid could do it because someone else is looking for him. Maybe that's why Finn was pushing so hard for us to find him."

I considered it and then shrugged. "At this point, any answer could be the right one. But if that's the case, don't you think Finn would've told us?"

Jacque frowned. "He's a mobster, Harry. He's only going to tell you what it suits him to tell you."

"Well," I said thoughtfully, "unfortunately until we have information from another source, we have to take him at face value, not to mention that he's the one footing the bill."

"I just don't like it," Jacque muttered.

"It's too late to change it now," I said with a chuckle as she followed me into the conference room.

"Good morning, everyone," I said, dumping my laptop onto the table.

"I'll get you some coffee," Jacque said.

"Thanks, Jacque," I said, then turned my attention to the group. "We have little time. Heather, we're wheels up at eleven, so we have to be out of here by nine-thirty—" I cut myself off as Jacque placed a steaming cup of black coffee in front of me.

"Ah, thank you," I said and looked up at her. "Oh, and we need hotel reservations in—"

"Already done," Jacque said, cutting me off. "I've also arranged a car and driver for you. I'll give you the details before you leave."

I grinned at her. "What a treasure you are."

"Get hold of yourself, Harry," she said, smiling. "We have work to do."

"That we do," I said and looked at Tim.

"I was able to gather a list of names," Tim said. "They're all acquaintances of the Rossi family, and the girlfriend. She seems to run in a different circle…" His voice trailed off in a way that caused me to frown.

"And can you expand on that?" I asked.

Tim sighed, rubbing his eyes beneath his glasses. "Well, see, that's the thing. I'm having a difficult time placing them all. And they're not good people. In fact, from what little I've been able to gather, my assumption is that the mother of Rossi's child has connections to the Italian mob."

"Oh, that's just terrific." I groaned, not bothering to hide my frustration.

"I don't know what to make of it," Tim said, "but I put together a list…" He picked up a printout and handed it to me.

I read the list of names, not recognizing a single one of them. I couldn't decide if that was a good or bad thing, and I didn't like it either way. This thing was already deteriorating into a hot mess.

"How about these people?" I asked. "Are any of them linked to... anything?"

"Uh..." Tim stepped over to me, pushed his new glasses up the bridge of his nose, leaned forward and glanced at the list. "This one," he said, pointing. "Enzo Massino. You should probably tread lightly with him."

"Why's that?" I asked.

"He's rumored to be the most powerful mob boss in New York City. I don't know if there's any truth to that, though," Tim added quickly. "That's just what I was able to pull from the dark web."

"How is he connected to Catherine?" Heather asked, speaking up. "Or any of them, I guess."

"Well, that's the thing," Tim said, his expression perplexed. "I don't really know. He just kept coming up anytime I searched for Catherine McCarthy. I don't know if she's related somehow —maybe distantly—or if they're friends?"

"That all?" I asked.

"Not quite." Tim nodded, then gestured to his computer and pulled up a picture. "This is them."

I stared at the image on the screen, noting the blond-haired, light-eyed woman. She was young, probably in her mid-twenties. The handsome man standing beside her, dressed in a suit and tie, was clearly Italian, his arm around her thin shoulders, his expression... stoney.

"He's younger than I expected," I said as I tried to guess the age of the rumored mob boss. "Maybe in his early to mid-thirties?"

"Yeah." Tim nodded. "His father, Vince Massino, passed away two years ago. It was at that point Enzo was rumored to have taken over the family business."

"Okay, that makes sense," I said. "Where'd you find this picture?"

"I dug it up on a server that had little protection. It was in Manhattan. I can give you the address if you'd like." Tim grabbed a piece of paper and a pen, then jotted down the address and handed it to me. I glanced at it, recognizing the upscale area.

"I wonder whose place this is," I thought aloud.

"It's owned by a property management company, so I don't know," Tim said. "I'm still working on it, though. I might have an answer for you soon."

I nodded, but then hesitated. Tim looked disheveled. I took in the fatigue lines around his eyes and realized he needed a break.

"You've done enough for today, Tim," I said. "Go home. Take the rest of the day off."

"No, no," he said, shaking his head.

"Harry's right," Heather said. "You look like hell, Tim. You've been working nonstop for almost two days. You have to give your body—and brain—a break."

"You do look pretty damn rough, son," TJ said and chuckled.

Tim's shoulders dropped, but I caught the look of relief. "Fine, I'll go home for a while, I guess."

"Good," I said. "And we're going to button everything up around here before Heather and I leave for what could be an extended stay." I knew Heather and I had our work cut out for us.

Thirty minutes later, Heather and I said our goodbyes and headed to the airport.

"This Enzo Massino," Heather said as we turned onto Wilcox Boulevard. "You think he really is a godfather?"

"Who knows?" I said, shaking my head. "I guess we'll find

out soon enough, though. If he is, it probably means this damn thing is mob related."

"I don't see how it could be anything other than mob related," Heather reasoned, leaning her head back against the rest. "It makes little sense for it to be anything else. There are connections to the Irish and the Italians. What would be the odds that it's *not*?"

"I'd say slim to none," I agreed. "But I still think Finn Doyle would've told us if he thought it was related to his business."

"But would he know if it was related to another family's business?" Heather asked. "We don't even know if Doyle has connections to any of the other families."

Heather had a point. Matteo could've been caught in the crossfire of a completely different war... Would Doyle have known about that? Maybe. Maybe not.

"I guess it'll be up to us to make that connection," I said thoughtfully.

"You think Doyle is back in New York City by now?"

I shrugged. "I don't think he's going to do any good hanging around Chattanooga. I wouldn't be surprised if he's waiting for us when we get there."

"Great," she said caustically. "I'm hoping he'll leave us alone to do our job. I'd hate to have someone with his reputation hanging over our shoulders, following us around. That could give someone the wrong idea."

I chuckled. "And what idea would that be, Heather? That we're working for him?"

She pursed her lips. "And why not? These people are born paranoid. There's no way to get around it, Harry. We've been hired by an Irish mob boss."

"Yep," I nodded. "And all we can do is hope we can keep that secret in our pocket."

9

WE TOOK OFF ON SCHEDULE AT ELEVEN O'CLOCK, AND I relaxed back in my seat, peering out into the wispy clouds. I'd grown accustomed to traveling in the Gulfstream, and now, the thought of cramming myself into a commercial aircraft made me cringe. I've never been one for luxury per se, but when it comes to travel, I am. It's expensive, and I don't get it for free, but the convenience more than offsets the cost.

"Two and a half hours, right?" Heather asked from the couch opposite.

I nodded. "Sounds about right. Maybe a little less."

She nodded, folded her arms, leaned her head back and closed her eyes.

I smiled and turned my attention back to the window, thinking about how valuable she was as a member of my team.

She was thirty-one when she came to work for me. At five feet eight inches tall, with short brown hair, an oval face, brown eyes, and a hard body she keeps well covered, she's an attractive woman. She spends an hour at the gym every morning, teaches Krav Maga self-defense in her spare time, and she's an expert shot.

DUPLICITY

She began her law enforcement career as an Atlanta beat cop. Two years later, she was recruited by the GBI (Georgia Bureau of Investigation) and was fast-tracked for high office, but something went wrong, something she never would talk about. I'd run into her frequently, both as a cop and a private investigator, and we'd formed a mutual respect.

Then, late one afternoon, she called me. She wanted to know if I had any openings. It so happened that I did. We were busy working seven days a week. I needed help, so I hired her. Why she left the GBI, I have no idea, but I suspect it was because of a personal relationship. Heather's gay, though as far as I knew, she's not in a relationship. Ten years on, she's my senior investigator.

I looked again at her. Her mouth was open a little, her head tilted slightly to one side; she was obviously asleep.

I chuckled to myself, realizing she had the right idea. So, I shut my eyes, took a deep breath, and let myself go.

I spent the rest of the flight slipping in and out of consciousness, though my brain never truly switched off. Even as I slept for the next two hours, my mind replayed Morrigan Doyle's case and the encounter Kate and I had in New York. By the time we landed at LaGuardia at a little after one that afternoon, I was feeling pretty antsy. If my gut was trying to forewarn me of what was to come, well, it was doing a good job of it.

"Hello, Mr. Starke," George, my father's driver, greeted me as the crew grabbed our bags and began loading them into the back of the SUV. "It's been a while."

"I suppose it has." I shook his hand. "This is Heather Stillwell, my associate."

"Nice to meet you, ma'am," George said, opening the back passenger door for us to slide in. Heather gave him a sweet smile and then we climbed into the back seat.

I settled in, then glanced at her. She seemed... unsettled. She'd said hardly a word since we landed.

"You're staying at the Hilton Garden Inn again, right?" George asked.

"Off Park Avenue," I clarified with a nod.

"Seems to be where you always stay when you're here in the city," he commented as he pulled out of the airport into dense traffic. I didn't mind the hustle and bustle of the Big Apple. I found the draw of the city intriguing—just as much as anyone else—but there was something to be said about the traffic. I hated it, and I knew by the time the trip was over, I'd be more than ready to be back home in Chattanooga.

Hell, I already was.

Heather spent the entire ride to the hotel looking out the window. And I wondered if it was her first time in the big city. I said nothing. Neither did she, and I wondered if this was how she was going to be the entire trip.

Inwardly, I shrugged. Heather was never the most talkative person.

I sat there for a moment, thinking, then I sent Amanda a text to update her.

Stay safe. Love you, she had replied. I smiled, already feeling a sense of longing to be home. Travel wasn't something I had to deal with often, but the older I got—and the older *Jade* got—the more I became attached to my life back home in Chattanooga.

The drive to the hotel took thirty-five minutes, and by the time we arrived, I was irritable and hungry. I told George to come back around three.

Jacque had booked two adjoining rooms, so while we had our privacy, we also had access to chat without having to go out into the hallway.

DUPLICITY

"I think we should start with Isabella Rossi," Heather announced as she stepped through the adjoining door.

I paused my unpacking. "Makes sense," I said.

Heather nodded. "From what I've gathered, she's always been close to her family, including her sons."

I looked at my watch. It was getting on for two-thirty, so I said, "George will be here in thirty minutes. Let's tentatively plan that we talk to the mother and call it a day. I'm not yet ready to foray into mob territory: Irish or Italian."

"Sounds good to me," Heather said, pulling out a notebook. "She lives in Bay Ridge. It's a nice house, albeit small, I think."

"Not a bad area," I agreed as I gathered my things, including my CZ75. I was hoping for the best, but I was always prepared for the worst. It was part of my survival instinct.

"We can grab dinner afterward," Heather said. "I'm really looking forward to getting started."

I chuckled. "At least one of us is." My phone beeped. I had a text. George was already outside waiting for us. The man was timely as ever, something I appreciated. He'd worked for my father for many years, and I was always grateful when he lent him to us.

"Should we take the photo?" Heather asked, hovering by the door. "The one of Matteo?"

I shrugged. "If your gut is telling you to bring it, then bring it." I spoke the words carefully, studying her face. She seemed more on edge than usual, and I had to wonder why.

"You okay?" I asked.

She adjusted her shirt. "Yeah. Like I said, I'm just ready to get started, see where this thing takes us. I have a feeling it's going to be bigger than we thought."

"Geez, I hope not," I muttered as I stepped out into the hallway, pulling the door closed behind me. Then, "Me, too," I said softly.

60

I wasn't sure if Heather heard me or not. If she did, she said nothing.

We took the elevator from the thirteenth floor down to the lobby in silence. I glanced at her several times. She seemed preoccupied.

We stepped out of the elevator, and I scanned the ornate lobby—another survival instinct—seeing nothing unusual. It was tourist time in New York City, and the lobby was packed with people and school kids out for the summer.

As we made our way to the driver, I paused outside the hotel bar. The smell of food was beyond tantalizing, and I realized just how hungry I was.

"Are you sure you don't want to grab something to eat before we get started?" I said.

Heather hesitated, made a face, then said, "George is waiting for us."

"I'm sure we could get something to go," I said, shrugging. "Besides, we don't know how long this interview with Isabella Rossi will last, or where it might lead. It could be late when we get finished." I really didn't think it would be, but I needed food.

Heather pursed her lips, narrowed her eyes, and then said, "Fine. Let's eat."

"Good," I said. "I'll send George a message and let him know we're grabbing something quick to eat."

Heather nodded. "I feel bad making him wait," she said.

"He's used to it," I replied. "He works for my father."

"Oh, yeah. I forgot." Heather laughed as we walked into the dimly lit room and took a seat at the bar.

"What can I do for you folks?" the bartender asked.

"Can we get something to eat?" Heather asked.

"Of course." He handed us a couple of menus. Then he

sauntered off to speak with a couple of young women at the far end of the bar.

"Well, I see he has his priorities," Heather said as she grabbed a menu and began flipping through it. Me? I opted to scan the room instead. It wasn't a large room, nor was it crowded. I looked out the window, seeing the passersby, all of them in a hurry, so it seemed. I shivered slightly, then turned my attention to the menu.

The bartender returned a couple of minutes later and we ordered burgers, fries, and two bottles of water.

Heather nudged me. "What did you see?"

I frowned. "See? What d'you mean?"

"You were staring out into the street and you had that look on your face, the one that tells me something isn't right." Heather picked up her bottle of water, opened it, and took a sip.

I shrugged, made a face, then said, "I don't know, Heather. It was just one of those gut feelings, as if we're being watched, but then again, this *is* New York City."

She nodded. "I suppose. It *is* kind of unnerving, though."

"Yes, it is," I agreed with her.

Our burgers arrived a few moments later and we ate them quickly, not wanting to keep George waiting any longer than we had to. That done, Heather asked for a bottle of water to go. I paid the bill, and we walked out onto the street where George was indeed waiting for us.

"Let's go see what Mrs. Rossi has to say," Heather said as she slid into the back seat.

Hopefully, she has a lot to say, I thought as I climbed in beside her.

10

THE SMALL HOUSE WHERE ISABELLA ROSSI LIVED ON SHORE Drive in the Bay Ridge area of Brooklyn was... quaint, though much nicer than I expected—at least on the outside.

George pulled up alongside the curb and let us out, saying he'd wait for us. I thanked him, and Heather and I walked up the steps to the front door.

"You sure this is it?" I asked as we stepped onto the small porch.

"Yep," Heather answered. "See?" She pointed to the doorbell and pushed the button. We could hear the chimes echoing through the house. I looked at her. She nodded, smiling, and we waited for someone to come to the door.

But they didn't.

After more than a minute, Heather looked at me. I nodded, and she rang the doorbell again, though I figured anyone in the house must have heard it the first time. And again, we waited, and we waited, until finally, just as I was about to give up, the door opened and a young woman with blond hair peered out at us.

"Yes," she said, her blue eyes flitting back and forth between us. "What can I do for you?" Her tone was sharp and not at all friendly. That being said, she obviously was *not* Isabella Rossi. She was, in fact, Catherine McCarthy, Matteo's girlfriend and the mother of his child.

"Good afternoon. My name's Harry Starke. I'm a private investigator. This is my associate, Heather Stillwell. We're here to see Mrs. Rossi… about her son."

"And we'd also like to talk with you, too," Heather added, her voice bright and amicable. "You *are* Catherine McCarthy, aren't you? I recognize you from your photograph."

Catherine looked at me, then at Heather, then at me again, as if she was trying to vet us.

"Okay. You must be the people Finny told me about." Her accent was broad Brooklyn. "You'd better come in then."

Finny? That's not quite how I see him, I thought as she stepped aside and opened the door to let us in.

I led the way. Heather followed close behind. The house was small and simply decorated: family photos on the wall, the furniture old, though well-cared for, and the place was impeccably clean and tidy.

"You can have a seat there." Catherine gestured to the chairs crammed around an old kitchen table, chipped and worn. "Isabella is just getting out of the shower. She'll be down soon. She didn't know you were coming."

"Finn didn't tell her?" I asked, frowning, still wondering about the way she'd spoken so casually about him. And I wondered what kind of relationship these people had with my client, and not simply because they were connected to the case. I needed to know Finn's character and how trustworthy a guy he really was.

"No, she's not speaking with him right now," Catherine answered, leaning her back against the bar in the kitchen, her arms folded, chin down, staring at us through those huge blue eyes. Her voice reminded me a little of Mona Lisa Vito in the movie *My Cousin Vinny*. "They have their ons and offs," she continued. "I think she blames him for getting Matty wrapped up in the mob."

I nodded, making a mental note, all the while hoping that Finn wouldn't be broadcasting to one and all that we were on the case.

"What can you tell me about Matteo's disappearance?"

Her lips twitched as she let out a long sigh. "I don't know much, and I've replayed the night over and over in my head. He was going out to the Palace, which is their nickname for the bar about five blocks from our apartment."

"You and Matteo's apartment?" I asked.

"Yes, it was ours. We hadn't been living there long. It just seemed easier to raise a child if we lived together, you know?" She paused, running her fingers through her hair. "We had some rocky times, though."

"What about that night?" I asked. "Was that one of those times?"

She locked eyes with me, stared at me for a moment, then said, "Yeah. That night we'd gotten into a fight. We have a kid, and sometimes it's hard to be on the same page. I was tired, and he had business to take care of. I wanted him to stay, and he wanted to go. Just like always," she said coldly.

"And so," I said, "just to be clear, you were angry with each other. He was angry when he went out. And that wasn't unusual?"

Catherine looked annoyed. "Yeah, I guess. We were going through another rough patch, but it wasn't gonna last. It never lasted. We always made up. Matty had a hard head sometimes, but he always came around. We never fought too long." Her voice softened. Her eyes welled up, with her hands now clasped together in front of her. "He never came home."

"Did he often stay out all night?" Heather asked, leaning back in her chair.

"Oh, uh..." Catherine hesitated. "Well, sometimes. Not often, though. It just depended on what, um, was going on, I guess. Sometimes he stayed out all night, but he was always home early the next morning. I knew that morning when he didn't come home, something was wrong. I can always get ahold of him. He always answers his phone. But I couldn't that morning. I called, and it went straight to voicemail."

"So, he *does* have a phone?" I asked, knowing that other than the phone he'd had years ago on his mother's plan, we'd found no evidence of him ever owning one.

"Yeah, everyone has a phone these days, don't they?" Catherine gave us a funny look. "He has a phone. Of course, he does."

"We were unable to find any record of him ever having a phone," I said. I needed to get into the fact that Matteo had no digital footprint, and I still wasn't sure that Catherine was being entirely truthful. She had an edge about her, and while it might just be the cold, hard city in her, I had to be sure.

"How would I know about that?" she snapped. "We don't share a phone bill, or anything. We only share the apartment. The guy is crazy. He doesn't want us to be connected. His name isn't on the lease, and I don't think there is anything that we share other than, you know, our son." Her tone dipped, and it was easy to see the frustration etched into her features. She was an attractive woman, but she was clearly distraught about Matteo, and I still wasn't sure it was his disappearance that was getting to her.

But then, what did I know? At that point, nothing for sure.

"Our baby was sick that night," she continued, shaking her head. "And I needed him to pick up some infant Tylenol. I sent him a bunch of texts and tried to call him. He didn't answer any of them. That's how I knew something was really wrong." She took a deep breath. "We might have been going through a rough patch, but he never failed our son. Ever. He's a good dad."

"And you don't think he could've just taken off?" I asked.

"No way," she answered immediately. "Absolutely not. If he took off, it would've been because he didn't have a choice. Matty didn't stand down from a fight, either. He never did." Catherine leaned forward and lowered her voice. "But listen, he *is* paranoid."

"Paranoid, you say?" Heather asked. "Why is he paranoid? Has he always been that way?"

Catherine nodded. "Absolutely. He's spent his entire adult life dodging and ducking the government, and it's not because he was in trouble or something. It's just how Matty is. He doesn't trust anyone, and he always thought that the government was responsible for the death of his father."

Whoa, wait. Hang on.

"What do you mean?" I asked. "What happened to his father?"

"Nothing that had to do with the government," a sharp voice said from the living room.

Heather and I looked round to see a dark-haired, petite woman walk into the kitchen. Her arms were folded across her chest, and her jaw was set tight, her chocolate eyes scrutinizing us. "You must be the private investigators Doyle hired."

Doyle. A far cry from Finny, I thought.

"We are," Heather answered. "Mr. Doyle hired us to find your son."

She pressed her thin lips together, warily glancing at Catherine. "Don't you have to go pick up Matty Junior from your mother?" There was a tenseness in her voice. It sounded to me as if Isabella wanted Catherine to leave.

Interesting dynamic between these two.

"I don't have to get him until six," Catherine responded softly. "I'd like to stay and chat with the detectives. I want to find Matty, too."

"I know you do," Rossi huffed, her olive-colored blouse hanging from her thin shoulders. She was a frail-looking woman, but something told me she wasn't so frail about the way she handled things.

She turned back to us and continued, "I don't have any information to give you other than that he was a good kid, until he got mixed up with Doyle and his crew. He's Italian, not Irish. What I mean to say is, he's an outcast."

"Why is that?" Heather asked.

Isabella glared at her. "I just told you; he's Italian... And they're Irish mob."

"I'd like to know more about his paranoia and his problems with the government," Heather said. "And we don't understand why he has no digital footprint. It's as if he hasn't existed for the past... ten years or more?"

"I can give you his phone number," Catherine offered. "But he changes it often. He uses pay-as-you-go phones. And he pays for everything with cash. He doesn't have no credit cards, bank account, or laptop, so no Facebook page or anything. And the phone companies... he thinks they're listening in to every word he says. I told you; he's paranoid, scared of every little shadow."

"You mentioned his father," I said. "Can you tell us what happened?

Isabella touched her face, which I took as a sign of being uncomfortable, her eyes going soft for just a moment, then shrugged. "It had nothing to do with the government. His father passed away on a jobsite of a heart attack. Nothing unusual. Matty refused to believe it, and so naturally, he thought he was murdered and that the medical examiner was corrupt. You see where I'm going." She stopped. "My son was in denial. He didn't think his tough father's heart could give out. But that's exactly what happened."

It felt like a stretch, but grief did occasionally cause strange reactions from loved ones, and I wondered if that was what happened to Matteo. He'd somehow manufactured a government conspiracy and shut himself off from the world, literally. And it was *really* working to his benefit now, given that he was just about impossible to trace.

"Listen, if you want to know what happened to him," Isabella said, "what we *all* think happened to him, you're going to have to talk to people who have connections with that shady crew he worked for. And not just the Irish… The…" She squeezed her eyes shut tight. "Enzo Massino is the head of an Italian family. I've known him all my life. They weren't happy about Matteo getting involved with Doyle and his mob. We all think he's responsible for Matteo disappearing."

Enzo Massino… Hmm.

"And that's all I have for ya." Isabella locked eyes with me. "I want to find my son," she said, "but I'm also terrified of *what* you might find."

I nodded, understanding what she was saying, and I empathized with her. It wasn't the first time I'd had to track down a wayward child. Sometimes it worked out well; other times? You don't want to know.

"And, so I understand it, you haven't contacted the authorities," I said. "Because you're assuming mob involvement."

"Didn't I just say so?" she snapped. "Of course, I am. And I know how these things play out, so I'd rather you not be loitering in my house any longer, Mr. Starke. I've nothing more to say to you. You can see yourselves out." And with that, she turned away and left the room, her long skirts swishing; an extension of her anger…? Or was it something else?

11

Catherine McCarthy grimaced as Isabella stalked out of the room, closing the door behind her.

"I'll show you out," she said.

"I'd like to see the apartment you share with Matteo," I said, rising to my feet.

She nodded, then said with a sigh, "Sure. I can meet you over there before I pick up my son. You'll just have to excuse Isabella. She's upset over what happened to Matty, and she's not happy with Finn right now. She doesn't trust him or anyone that works for him."

"We never got the chance to ask her if Matteo has any enemies, anyone who might want to hurt him," Heather said, frowning.

"Hah! Take your pick," Catherine answered. "He works for Finn, doesn't he?" She paused, then continued. "He isn't really the kind of guy who picks fights with anyone. He does his job, and that's where it ends. Most of the people he works with like him, but the Italians... I don't know. I never really knew anything."

"What about Enzo Massino?" I asked as we stepped outside onto the stoop.

"I don't know nothing about that," she replied. "I just know Massino isn't the kind of guy you'd want to go poking around. He's not going to be forthcoming, especially if he knows you were hired by Finn."

"Isabella said she's known him for a long time?" Heather said. "Do you know anything about that?"

"No, Matty isn't the kind of guy who talks about his past." She shrugged. "You want my apartment address, then?"

I nodded. She tapped it into her phone and sent it to me My phone pinged. The apartment was in Hell's Kitchen, off West 47th. "Got it," I said. "We can give you a ride over there, if you'd like."

Catherine looked uneasily at the SUV. "Um... Okay. Yeah, that's fine." She fell silent as we made our way to the car. I got into the passenger seat while Heather and Catherine climbed in behind.

I gave George the address, and he punched it into the GPS.

"How long have you been with Matty?" Heather asked.

"Oh, a while now," she said. "We aren't the type of couple to keep up with the time, but I've known him for about five years now, I guess. We met when I was at Columbia."

Columbia? Geez. How'd she manage that?

"Is your family from the city?" I asked.

"No. I grew up in Boston, and then I came here to Columbia. I didn't finish, though. I fell in with Matty and dropped out. I wasn't doing well, anyway. Made my parents really mad. That's where I've been ever since. I got pregnant, and that's when we decided to move in together. It's just what had to happen. I couldn't afford to live alone, and if I was going to have a roommate, it might as well be my boyfriend." She sounded... almost detached from what she was saying.

Maybe that's how she's coping, I thought. *After all, Matteo Rossi's been missing for more than a month, so it makes sense that the edge has worn off.*

"Do you get along with Isabella?" Heather asked softly. "You both seemed a little tense."

Catherine laughed. "We get along just fine, really. Isabella is just the typical Italian woman living in Brooklyn, ya know? She comes off a little spicy, I suppose, but her heart's in the right place. She loves Matty, and she's having to deal with losing him, and that hasn't been easy for her. Not to mention, Micah is in trouble again."

"What for?" I asked, knowing the charges were assault and battery, but I wanted to hear it from her.

"He got into a fight with some guys down at the Palace," she replied. "It wasn't anything much, just another night out for Micah. He's a hothead, and it's always gotten him in trouble. And Matty isn't here to smooth things out for him anymore."

"So Matty looked out for him, then?" I asked.

"Yeah, I guess," she replied thoughtfully. "I think it was a relief to Matty when Micah was locked up, though. It meant he didn't have to worry about him as much, you know? He just had to make sure he had money, and so on."

"Right," Heather said. "I get that. But do you think Micah's fight had anything to do with what happened to Matty?"

"No. I don't think so," she replied. "I think he was probably just blowing off steam. He was worried about Matty, of course, but he wasn't looking for him... At least, I don't think he was. We all know how things work around here..." She trailed off, then said, "We don't ask questions."

"But Finn does," I said.

"Yeah. Him and Matty are best friends. Matty was closer to Finn than Micah ever was. Finn wants answers, and what Finn

DUPLICITY

wants, he gets. He won't stop until he finds out what happened to his best friend."

"Here we are," George said as he pulled up to the curb and put the car in park.

"Thanks, George," I said. "We won't be long."

"You got it." George gave me a thumbs up as I stepped out onto the street and looked up at the dingy high-rise apartment building with its fire escapes decorating the walls.

The area was a little rougher than the spot where Isabella lived, but overall, it wasn't the worst part of the city.

"Follow me," Catherine said as she led the way. "Oh, and the bar, the Palace, is just five blocks that way. It doesn't have a sign out front or anything. You gotta take the alley to get in But you can tell them that Finn sent you. They won't kick you out, I don't think." She looked uncertain but then shook her head and led us to a first-floor apartment.

Heather and I waited as she punched a code into the door lock. The lock clicked and she opened the door, stepped inside and flipped on the lights, and then stood aside for us to enter what I could already see was a *tiny* apartment.

"It's a bit of a mess," Catherine said, standing out of the way. "I haven't had a lot of time to clean, what with suddenly becoming a single mom, you know?" Her cheeks blushed crimson as we stepped further into the tiny apartment, stepping over and around baby toys.

"It's got a nice terrace," Heather said, peering out through the glass door. "It's lovely."

"Thank you. Matty loved sitting out there, smoking," Catherine said, her voice faltering slightly. She quickly recovered and looked away. "Anyway, you guys look around all you want. I don't have anything to hide. He didn't have an office or anything like that. I would say if he had one, it would be the Palace." Her tone had soured, and I glanced at Heather.

I already knew we'd be paying the Palace a visit. It was the last place Matteo had been seen, and I knew that someone, somewhere, knew something. Now, whether or not they would talk to us... Well, that was yet to be determined.

Heather slid open the glass door and stepped out onto the terrace. Catherine followed, and soon the two of them were talking easily together.

I took advantage of the moment and went into the first bedroom off the living area. To say it was tiny would be an understatement. It was little more than a closet, and the only furniture was a crib and a small chest of drawers. I took a quick look around but saw nothing of interest.

The master bedroom—if you could call it that—wasn't much bigger; just the bare minimum of furniture: a queen-size bed, a dresser, a dining room chair and a small table, and it didn't take me but a minute to realize that Matteo kept *nothing* there. And I do mean nothing. It was as if the man didn't live there. I did find a second toothbrush in the small bathroom and a couple of pairs of men's jeans and a shirt in a cupboard. Other than that... *Nothing.*

I went back into the living room and out onto the terrace.

"Catherine," I said. "Where are all Matteo's belongings? There's almost nothing here."

Her cheeks reddened. "His mother came and got most of his stuff a couple of weeks ago. I don't know why, but I didn't stop her. It's as if she wanted it for herself. She said she wanted to go through his things."

"But there's no proof that anything happened to—"

"To Isabella, there is," Catherine said, cutting Heather off. "The minute I told her he didn't come home that night, she thought it was over. She said she just knew it in her gut."

Or she knew it because she knows more than she's telling, I thought.

DUPLICITY

"Anyway," Catherine continued. "I need to get over to my mother's. I have to pick up my son."

"I thought you said your family wasn't from New York?" I asked, catching the inconsistency.

"We're not." Catherine frowned at me. "My parents still live in Boston, but they bought an apartment in Chelsea after the baby was born. They want to be as involved as possible, so they come and stay pretty often. They wanted me to move back home, and when I refused, they bought the apartment."

"Fair enough," I said, making a mental note that maybe we should add her parents to the list of people to talk to. The list was growing, and I was beginning to wonder if I should have brought TJ with us after all.

I took a deep breath. *One step at a time, Harry. One step at a time.*

12

THE PALACE WASN'T HARD TO LOCATE, GIVEN THAT Catherine's directions led us to an alleyway five blocks to the north of her apartment. It was just another hole-in-the-wall kind of dive bar—no different from most of the bars in and around New York City.

"I wonder what kind of a crowd this place caters to," Heather muttered as we walked together down the alley to a flight of four steps leading to a black door with the word *Palace* painted in red.

"I doubt they'll be the kind that will welcome a couple of private investigators from Chattanooga," I replied and chuckled as we took the steps up to the door.

The door didn't have a knob, so I pushed on it and it swung open, providing access to an unsurprisingly dimly lit bar. The room was thick with cigarette smoke, a den of iniquity if ever I saw one.

There were maybe a dozen people seated around the room and a bartender leaning against the counter. He spotted us the moment we stepped inside and scowled.

"Can I help ya?" he called out as we made our way across the room to the bar.

"I hope so," I said, thinking it all reminded me a little of the Sorbonne back in Chattanooga, a place I'd barely set foot in since Benny Hinkle was murdered more than a year ago.

Heather slid onto one of the stools at the far end of the bar so she could keep an eye on things.

"What the hell do you want?" the bartender snapped. "You guys reek of cop."

His red hair was fiery like the sun beating down on the concrete outside, and his eyes, mere slits, were green as grass, and I wondered if he was as Irish as he looked.

"Well, we're *not* cops," I said, with a smile I didn't feel. "We're working for Finn Doyle, and we're looking for a little help. Do you happen to know this fella?" I nodded to Heather, and she pulled out the snapshot, holding it out for him to see.

His expression changed. I could tell he recognized him. And I waited to see if he was going to be forthcoming. He took the photo from her and squinted at it.

"That's Matteo," he said, handing it back to Heather. "Where'd you get it? It was taken in here. Right over there, in fact." He gestured to a spot near the jukebox.

"We got it from Finn Doyle," I said. "We're trying to find Matteo."

"Well, Matty ain't been in for his shift in more than a month. He got off work after a Friday night shift and then never showed back up."

"He worked here?" I frowned.

The guy sighed. "Yeah, he did. I'm Frank Palace. I own this place. He's worked here since he was legal. Paid him in cash because he's strange about the government... or something. But yeah. Wasn't like him to skip a shift, but if you saw the guys he ran with... Well, you know. I know what he was involved with."

I nodded, took out my phone, typed in *Frank Palace, Palace bar, W 47th,* and sent it to Tim. "So you didn't think to report him missing?" I asked.

"Me?" he said, his eyebrows raised in surprise. "Why would I do that? He just worked here. And, like I said, I know what he was mixed up in, an' I don't have no death wish. My customers are loyal, but only to a point."

"Do you know any reason why he might want to disappear?" Heather asked, frowning, still holding the photograph of Matteo Rossi.

Frank hesitated for a moment, then reached down and came up with a couple of glasses. "What'd you want to drink?"

"I'm good, thanks," Heather said.

"I'll have a Jameson on the rocks," I said, not wanting to offend him.

He eyed me but then turned away to make the drink.

"Matty wasn't a troublemaker," he said with his back to me, "and if it weren't for Finn Doyle, I don't think he would've ever gotten into the kind of underworld crap he did. He could've been a lot more, but that girlfriend of his..." His voice trailed off, and he shook his head. "She's bad news."

"Why's that?" I asked, a little confused. Catherine McCarthy didn't seem to me to be anything more than a fairly ordinary young mother.

"I just knew," he said. "She pushed him, y'know? He picked up extra shifts after they got into it big time. Like he wasn't makin' enough money for her. Like she wanted fancy and shit. But see, Matty was just a mule for Finn and a part-time bartender here. He wasn't some high-rankin' mafia guy. He didn't do a bunch of dirty work and wasn't in on the know. But she wanted him to be."

"For money?" Heather asked, nursing the glass of water

Frank placed in front of her. "I mean, couldn't he have gotten a better job?"

"Yeah, right!" Frank scoffed. "I told you; he's low on the pole. Low-level guys in the business don't make a bunch of money. He has no education to speak of, and maybe if he would've stuck it out with me, well, maybe we'd both get somewhere. It's not like I'm getting rich, either."

"Hmm…" I tapped my fingers on the bar, trying to put it together. "What about that night? Did anything unusual happen?"

"Uh, nope. Not really," he said with a shrug. "We closed up at the usual time, and then after we locked up, we stepped outside together. There were some guys—three of them—waiting for him in the alley. They looked kind of shady, but then they all look shady around here, you know? That's Hell's Kitchen for ya."

I nodded. "Did you recognize any of them?"

"No, I didn't," Frank answered, his voice flat. "I have no idea who they were. Hadn't ever seen them in here. If I had… well, I know my customers." The look he gave us made it clear how he felt about us. We didn't belong there.

"What about the days leading up to that night?" Heather asked. "Any phone calls? Any troubles with any of your customers that involved Matteo? How about you? Where did you go after you left him that night?"

"That's a mouthful of questions, lady," he replied. "But nope! Nothing that was out of the ordinary. Like I said, I knew him and his girl had gotten into a hell of a fight, but he didn't talk about it. Not much, anyway. But it bothered him. I could tell just by looking at his face. Other than that, I can't think of anything. That night was the last time anyone seen him." Frank frowned. "And where was I that night? I can't believe you're askin' me, but if you're asking for an alibi, when I left Matty that night, I went over to my friend's house. Her name's Rebekah Carter."

I nodded. "How about security footage?"

Frank tipped his head back and laughed. "Oh no, no, no. There ain't no cameras around here. That's the reason my place is a hot spot for a certain type of people."

I nodded, and as I did, my phone began to buzz in my pocket. I took it out and looked at the lock screen, hoping to see Amanda's name and face, but it was a New York number, one I didn't recognize.

"Hello."

"Mr. Starke?" The voice was deep, the accent Brooklyn.

"Yes?" I said, looking at Heather, who was watching me curiously as Frank stepped out from behind the bar to greet a couple of customers.

"This is Enzo Massino," the voice said. "I hear you're wanting to chat?" His tone was icy but with a tinge of amusement.

"I would," I said. "I'd like—"

"I know what it's about," he said, cutting me off. "My office. Ten o'clock tomorrow morning, sharp. I'll send the address to this number." And with that, he hung up. I took the phone away from my ear, looked at the blank screen, shook my head, and sighed. *Typical mafia don. What the hell am I doing here?*

"We need to go," I said to Heather as I sent George a text. I'd told him not to wait around out on the street.

She nodded to Frank as he returned behind the bar and said, "Thank you for your time, Frank. You've been a big help. If you think of anything else, please let us know." She handed him a card as we stood up to leave. I added a twenty-dollar tip and then we made our way out of the bar. I sent Jacque a text, letting her know we were calling it a day.

DUPLICITY

Barely had I hit send when my phone buzzed with a message from George. He was on his way and would meet us at the entrance to the alley.

"That was George," I said, glancing at Heather, and I stopped in my tracks. Something was wrong, and it was written all over her face.

13

"WE'RE BEING FOLLOWED," HEATHER SAID QUIETLY, JUST LOUD enough for me to hear. "There are three men behind us. They were hanging out by the jukebox."

I sighed, angry with myself that I hadn't paid attention to what was going on in the bar; it wasn't like me to be so lax. We stepped out of the alley onto the street and stopped walking. I called George.

"Where are you?" I asked.

"Not far. What's the hurry?"

"We're being followed," I replied.

"I'm on Forty-seventh, Harry," he said, his voice chipper. "I can see you."

"Good," I said and hung up, stuffing the phone into my jacket pocket.

"They're closing in on us," Heather said.

I glanced over my shoulder. She was right: three men wearing hoodies, all with their hoods up and heads low. It wasn't a good sign, but what did it mean? Were they headed in the same direction we were? Maybe. Maybe not.

Either way, I wasn't taking any chances. I grabbed Heather's wrist and tugged her out into the street, ignoring the honking horns as we weaved our way to the black SUV some fifty feet away.

I looked back over my shoulder as I flung the rear door open. Sure enough, they were following us out into traffic.

"Get in, Heather," I snapped. She did, and I jumped in after her.

"Let's go, George," I shouted.

He stomped on the gas, throwing us back in our seats, as he whipped out and around the taxi in front of him.

"I don't think those boys were up to any good," George commented with a light laugh as he took a hard left.

I peered out the back window as we made the turn, but they seemed to have disappeared.

"I don't know if they were or not," I said. "What I do know is I don't want them following us back to the hotel. I'm not sure if they overheard our conversation or if they were just planning to rough us up a little."

Part of me wanted to turn around and talk to Frank again. I was pretty sure he must know who they were. However, I wasn't sure what good it would do. We were only hours into the investigation, and I still didn't know what we were up against. And, at that point, I didn't want to push my luck.

It was just after eight and still light when George dropped us off at the Hilton, tired and more than a little frazzled.

"I don't know what to make of any of this," Heather said as we stepped into the elevator. "So, Matteo had a job at the bar. Why wouldn't Catherine have mentioned that? From what Frank said, she obviously knows."

I shook my head. "Maybe she didn't know. Maybe he didn't want her to know. We need to talk to her again and find out."

"But she knew he worked for Doyle," Heather said.

"Maybe... I don't know," I replied. "Maybe Frank's full of

it. Maybe he has ulterior motives. He was pretty damn aggressive when we walked in there. Then he loosened up and started talking. We don't know who this Frank guy is, and we don't know if we can trust him. Maybe he was making it up?"

"Why would he make up that Matteo worked there?" Heather asked as the elevator doors opened. "It would make no sense... unless that's how he covers for the guys?"

We stepped out of the elevator. I shrugged. "It's possible, I suppose..."

Heather was on a roll. I could almost see the wheels turning in her head as she started back up again, working through our visit to the Palace. "And what about the three guys he said were waiting for Matteo when he left that night? Frank said he didn't recognize them. I find that hard to believe. Don't you? And..." she continued, "could they have been the same three men who followed us tonight?"

"Maybe," I said and frowned, wondering if they were and if they had anything to do with his disappearance.

I opened the door to my room and Heather followed me in. We'd left the adjoining door open.

Heather dropped into one of the armchairs.

"I assume you texted Tim," she said. "Any word on Frank Palace?"

"Not yet," I said after checking my texts. "But I have no doubt that he'll get back to me as soon as he knows something. Look, I think we should call it a night. I'm bushed. We'll have breakfast and start again in the morning."

"Sounds good," Heather said, standing up again. "I'll come knocking around eight."

I nodded. "I'll be ready. Have a good night, Heather."

She nodded, gave me a smile, and then slipped through into the adjoining room, closing the door and locking it behind her.

I plugged my cell phone into the charger and then took a quick shower; that's where I often do my best thinking.

I couldn't help but wonder about the three men who followed us out of the bar. Maybe I'd made a mistake by not confronting them.

And where the hell is Finn Doyle?

The question popped into my head, and once there, it stayed late into the night.

I didn't sleep well that night. I went to bed still pondering the whereabouts of Finn Doyle. Could he have hired those people to follow us? It wouldn't have surprised me. And what about Enzo Massino? How did he know we wanted to talk to him?

Isabella Rossi, I thought. *That's how. She must have reached out to Massino. She said she knew him. How deep does that relationship go? Maybe deeper than she let on.*

Italian mob, Irish mob... Are they rivals? Or are they partners?

I had more questions than answers. My initial assumption was that the two factions weren't friends. However, the times they were a-changing, to paraphrase Bob Dylon, so it was impossible to know... *Hmm, maybe Enzo Massino can provide some answers.*

It was as I lay there, staring at the ceiling, that my phone began to vibrate on the nightstand. I looked at the clock. It was just after eleven. I picked up the phone, glanced at the screen, and wasn't surprised to see it was Tim.

"Hey," I said. "Isn't it past your bedtime?"

Tim laughed, then said, "I suppose it is, but I still have things to do. And I thought you'd like to talk about Frank Palace."

I sat up, swung my legs out of bed and rested my elbows on my knees, my phone at my ear.

"Go ahead, Tim?"

"Well, that's the thing..." His voice trailed off for a moment, then he said, "How can I put this? Hmm. I don't think that's who you talked to. From what little I've been able to find out so far, Frank Palace is another ghost. He doesn't exist."

"What?" I said—probably too loud with Heather sleeping in the next room—and sat up straight. "That can't be right. He's the bartender and owner of the Palace off West Forty-seventh."

"Yeah, so he might be, but his name's not Frank Palace. The registered owner of that building is Romeo Necesaro, and the Palace basement bar is... well, it doesn't exist either. I know, I know," he said before I could interrupt him. "You were in there, talking to *someone*. But if you were talking to the owner, his name's Romeo Necesaro, not Frank Palace, and there's no record of the bar either. If it exists, it exists under the radar."

"Okay, I get it," I said. "But I was there. There has to be something."

"Oh, there is on the dark web," Tim replied. "It's a hot spot for the underworld, a place where people can meet up for... let's say to make business transactions."

"Like drug dealing?"

"No," Tim answered flatly. "Not at all. It seems to be much darker than that; think trafficking, con artists, hitmen, mobsters."

"Palace, or whoever he was, told us that Matteo Rossi worked there as a bartender," I said. "Anything about that?"

"It's impossible to say." I heard him sigh. "Rossi is still a dead end, a ghost. He could have been working there or... anywhere. Who's to know? Maybe that's the story they tell when someone comes looking for him."

"Maybe."

"But listen, there is one thing," Tim said. "There was a

Frank McGrath who lived in that building until about four months ago."

"*Lived?*" I asked. "Where is he now?"

"Don't know," Tim replied. "He seems to have dropped off the map, too."

"You think he might be dead?"

I could almost see him shaking his head. "I don't know, Harry. Maybe. But he could be the guy you talked to. That bar is really shady."

"Whew... That's a lot of unknowns you've handed me, Tim," I said, my elbows on my knees again, my eyes shut tight. "This is crazy," I said, after a moment of silence. "Keep digging. We need to find something we can use. In the meantime, we have a meeting with Enzo Massino tomorrow morning at ten."

"Oh boy." Tim laughed. "Now you're talking. That man has a rap sheet a mile long, Harry. He's Italian mafia. He took over the family business when his father passed, and he hasn't looked back. He's into just about everything: prostitution, drugs, money laundering. For some reason I don't think he's into trafficking, but I could be wrong. As far as I can tell, he has no connection to the Irish, but again, I could be wrong."

"Another unknown, I think," I said, glancing wearily at the clock. "Well, one thing we do know is that there's a connection between Isabella Rossi and Massino, though just what that connection might be is another question we don't have an answer to."

"Well, I guess maybe you'll be able to figure it out tomorrow."

I sure hope so.

"Yeah, maybe. Good night, Tim. Go home and get some rest." And with that, I hung up and got back into bed.

14

I closed my eyes, but sleep didn't come until well after two, which is the last time I remember looking at the clock. My mind was in turmoil. What had I gotten myself into? Who was Frank Palace? Who was Frank McGrath? The three guys that followed us out of the bar. Finn Doyle... Finn Doyle? That name revolved around and around inside my head. What was he really up to? What was his motivation? Had he lied to me? Enzo Massino? Catherine McCarthy? She lied to me. Why, and so it went on and on and on...

It was five after six when I woke that following morning feeling like I had been run over by a road roller. I stared at the clock for several seconds, contemplating what I wanted to do first. It was still too early to call Amanda.

My mouth felt like the bottom of a parrot cage. I swallowed hard, sat up, and flipped back the covers, thinking it would be better to pound the pavement in Central Park rather than lie in bed stewing. So I dragged myself out of bed, put on my sweats and headed for the elevators.

I was out the door by five-thirty. Central Park was just a mile and a half away, and I was in the park and on the pond side pathway within twenty-five minutes and on my way around the pond. The air was heavy. The sun was peeking through the treetops. It was a pleasant morning and, early as it still was, there were a lot of people out there walking and running.

Running without headphones, or in only one ear, has always been my norm, choosing to hear the surrounding sounds rather than the music throbbing in my ears. But that wasn't the only reason. Running without headphones ensured no one could come up on me without me knowing it. Crazy, huh? You think I'm paranoid... Well, maybe I am, and with good reason. I'd spent a lifetime warding off shady characters and criminals. And remember, we'd already been followed by three shady characters, and there was no telling who might be watching me. I laughed to myself at the thought as a bead of sweat rolled down my cheek.

A soft breeze was blowing through the trees, and I sucked in a huge breath of the momentary fresh air. Central Park is a world unto itself, an oasis of green in the middle of the towering city. The air seems fresher there, and you feel a little closer to nature, something you wouldn't think possible amid all the concrete and glass.

And so I jogged steadily around the lake toward the exit that would take me back to Park Avenue and the hotel, once again lost in thought.

I turned left toward the exit and... *Whoa!* I slammed to a stop, recognizing the face of the man sitting on the bench.

Frank Palace...

His green eyes locked onto mine. He looked startled. Then he jumped to his feet and took off at a dead run.

Oh no, no, no. You're not going anywhere, bud.

My muscles were warm, and I was probably in the best shape I'd been in months. I leaped forward after the redheaded man. I watched, smiling, as he dodged and swerved to avoid the other runners and walkers. Me? I ran after him at an easy pace, and slowly, I caught up with him.

I grabbed his shirt at the back of his neck and took him down, hard.

"What the hell?" he gasped as he rolled over onto his back, trying to wriggle out of my grasp.

"Gotcha," I snapped. "Who the hell *are* you, buddy? You're surely not Frank Palace."

There was little reaction. The man's face was set in a grimace. I didn't know if he was hurt or just pissed off. Whatever it was, I kept him pinned to the ground, my knee on his gut, ignoring the onlookers and their ever-ready cell phones, and concentrated on Frank. I put a little more weight on his stomach; he winced.

"Get off me," he yelped.

"Not until you give me some answers," I snapped. "Was anything you told me last night the truth?"

"Yeah, yeah, it was," he squeaked, his face contorted with pain from the pressure of my knee in his gut. "Lemme up. I can't breathe," he gasped. "Just let me up and I'll talk to you. I swear."

I lifted my knee just enough for him to suck in a breath. "Okay," I said. "Start talking."

"Let me up first," he whispered. "I can't breathe."

I stared down at him. "Okay, but if you run, we're just going to repeat it, but this time I'll hurt you."

"I gotcha. Just get off me."

I eased up on him and stepped away, watching him.

He sat up, sucking in air. He rolled his shoulders and then his neck, blinked several times, then looked at me and said, "I was here to meet someone."

"Who?" I asked.

DUPLICITY

"I don't know," he said, squinting and making a face. "I'm just the delivery guy."

"Get up," I snapped.

He rose slowly to his feet.

"What're you delivering?" I asked.

"Nothing to do with Matty," he said, his chest heaving. "And I'm sure the client's split by now. It's not a good look for me to be chased through Central Park."

"All right, Frank, or whatever your name is, let's start over. Who the hell are you? You're not Frank Palace."

"That would be correct." He half chuckled as he walked along beside me. "But I go by Frank Palace. My real name is nobody's business but mine. And I do run the bar. I don't own it, though, and I don't own the building."

"And Matteo Rossi?"

He glanced sideways at me warily, then nodded and said, "Matty was my friend, and he did work shifts at the bar to earn some extra cash. Look…" He put a hand on my arm, stopped walking, turned to me and continued. "He's a good guy, Mr. Starke, and I don't know what he's gotten himself mixed up in. I make it a point to keep my nose out of what goes on there. That way I get to keep my fingers."

I locked eyes with him, still not sure if he was telling the truth. "Tell me about the night he went missing," I said. "You told me there were three guys waiting for him outside in the alley."

He nodded. "And that's the truth. There were three of them, and no, I don't know who they are. I don't know nothing about them. I just know that Matty seemed to know them, seemed to be friendly with them. It didn't look like anything bad… or anything. I figured they were some of Finn's guys. His guys are always comin' around."

"What d'you know about a guy named Frank McGrath?"

Frank's brows furrowed. "Nothin', why?" he replied.

"You should. He lived in your building. He went missing about four months ago."

"There's a lot of people who live in that building," he replied. "None of 'em come into my bar that I know of..." He trailed off, staring at me, then he got it and said, shaking his head, "Oh, no. I'm not him, if that's what you're thinking. It would be pretty stupid to change only my last name. Maybe McGrath's one of Finn Doyle's guys. If he is, I ain't heard nothing about him. The guy could've just split, you know?"

"Right," I said. "So what's your real name, Frank?"

He frowned. "You're a cop, so I ain't tellin' you nothin'."

"I'm *not* a cop, Frank. I'm a private investigator. I'm just trying to find Matteo, so give: what's your name?"

"Dylan Thomas," he whispered. "Like the poet. That's my real name. I had to change it because I was an accessory to a... Yeah, well, anyway, that doesn't matter, does it? The point is, Mr. Starke, I don't know what happened to Matty, but I wouldn't be surprised if he..." His voice trailed off.

"If he, what?" I said as my phone buzzed in my pocket. "Hold on a minute." I took it out and glanced at the screen. It was Amanda. I let it go to voicemail and said, "Go on, Frank."

"I think Matty was in trouble," he said, and it didn't surprise me. "I don't know with who or why, or... what. Things seemed to be going well for him, from what I could tell. He didn't have any beef with Doyle's crew. He was doing what he was supposed to be doing."

"Doing what?" I asked.

"I told ya," he yapped. "I keep my nose outa what don't concern me."

I nodded. "What about rivals?"

Frank made a face, wrinkled his forehead and said, "What about them?"

"The Italians," I said. "Could they have had anything to do with Matteo's disappearance? You know what happens when they want to make a point."

"Nah." He shook his head. "Not Matty. Maybe that's what happened to Frank McGrath, but not Matty. He wasn't worth nothin' to anyone when it came to the families."

"You say that, but wasn't he Finn Doyle's best friend?" I asked as I typed a quick text to Amanda, letting her know I'd call her back in a few minutes.

"Uh…" His voice trailed off. "Is that what Finn said?" I studied the man's face, and by his expression, I knew he wasn't going to be straight with me about anything concerning Finn Doyle. I realized he was scared of the Irish don and wasn't going to cross him. "They were close, yeah," he finally answered, looking away to his left, a sure sign he was lying.

I nodded, knowing there was little more to be gotten out of him.

"What else can you tell me?" I asked, knowing it was a stupid question.

And, sure enough, he shook his head, avoided eye contact with me and said, "It's a mystery where Matty went. I wish I hadn't gone to my friend's place that night. I wish I'd seen what those guys wanted with him, who they were, even, but I didn't want to come across as nosy, you know? It'll get you killed. But I do know he wouldn't have taken off unless it was bad. He was all about his kid, even if his lady wasn't a fan."

"She said they were having a tough time," I said.

"That's an understatement." He chuckled. "Look, I have to go. I need to find my guy. I don't want to end up missing, Mr. Starke. Have a nice day." And with that, he took off jogging toward a young woman in running gear.

I watched as they embraced, and while I was curious, I

wasn't so curious I wanted to pry; though I did wonder who she was and what she was to Frank.

Another question for another day, I thought as I turned and walked away.

I hadn't expected to run into Frank Palace that morning—or Dylan Thomas, as he said—and I wasn't sure there was any truth in anything he told me.

I stopped walking and stood for a moment, thinking, of what, I can't remember, but I do remember I glanced at my phone and saw I had a text from George, letting me know he'd pick us up at nine-thirty sharp. That being so, I needed to get a move on if I was going to have time to shower, eat, and call Amanda before we headed to Wall Street to meet with Enzo Massino.

15

I called Amanda on my way back to the hotel and caught up on how things had been going, and I had a quick word with Jade.

Back at the hotel, I showered, dressed in a pair of dark wash jeans, a plain white T-shirt, and my blue suit jacket. I was slipping my CZ into its holster under my arm when there was a knock at the door and Heather stepped in.

"Well, good morning," I said. "You about ready? George will be here at nine-thirty, so we're going to have to be quick with breakfast."

"Then I suggest we hit the Starbucks downstairs," she said with a grin.

I shrugged. "Fine with me. Let's get a move on. I've already had quite a morning, by the way."

"Oh?" Heather raised her eyebrows at me as we stepped out into the hallway. "Do tell."

And I did. I filled her in as we made our way down to the lobby and Starbucks. I told her about my conversation with Tim and the one I'd had with the man who called himself Frank Palace. Heather listened intently, nodding along until I finished.

"Wow," she said as we stepped into the line. "That's really something. Have you had a chance to send his real name to Tim yet?"

"Yep. I sent him a text after I got off the phone with Amanda. Told him about running into Frank in the park. The man's an enigma. I'm almost sure he was spinning me another bag full of lies. He's scared witless by Finn Doyle, and I have to wonder why. He sure as hell didn't want to talk about him. Is he a crook? Almost certainly. Is he a danger to society? I don't think so."

"Hmm..." She placed her index finger against her chin. "Maybe he's not, but I have a feeling the man we're about to meet is."

"You're probably right," I said as we shuffled forward.

We both ordered a blonde latte. I also ordered a croissant breakfast sandwich, and Heather ordered a plain bagel with cream cheese.

I checked my watch and seeing that it was only ten past nine and we still had twenty minutes before George was scheduled to arrive, we settled down to eat breakfast.

"You know," I said before taking a sip of my coffee, "there's something I can't quite shake. Frank—or whatever his name is—didn't react the way I thought he would when I mentioned that Finn and Matty were close."

Heather nodded, swallowed, and then said, "Okay, but now that we know nothing about this guy is kosher, what does it matter? As you said, he's an enigma. Catherine also said that Matteo and Finn were close. Plus, he was in most of the family pictures."

"True," I agreed. "But he also said that Catherine and Matteo weren't on good terms, either. In fact, if he's to be believed, they were close to the end of their ropes. He also said that Matteo was in good standing with the Irish."

Heather frowned. "It's just one contradiction after another. Is there anyone we can trust? I don't think so." She sighed, then said, "None of what we've learned so far is helpful."

"I agree," I said. "Maybe this mafioso will clarify things for us."

I took one last bite of my sandwich and then stood up. "C'mon," I said. "George should be here by now, and we don't want to keep him waiting."

Sure enough, George was waiting outside when we stepped out onto the street.

He held the rear door open for us, and two minutes later we were heading along FDR Drive toward the financial district.

∼

"TEXT ME WHEN YOU'RE READY," George said as we left the car.

I nodded, thanked him, and gave him a wave as he drove away. Then I turned to Heather and said, "You ready for this?"

"Let's do it," she said as we stepped through the revolving doors into a large, somewhat austere lobby. The silence after the morning traffic out on the street was almost palpable.

We paused for a moment, looked around, then took the elevator to the seventh floor in silence.

The elevator chimed, and the doors opened onto a wide hallway with glass doors on either side. Massino's office was two doors down on the left, and when I say office, it was, in fact, a small suite of offices. I pushed the door open and stood aside for Heather to enter first.

"Good morning," a young, sharply dressed woman seated at a small desk said. "You must be the private investigators Mr. Massino is expecting." She was smiling, but her tone was less than friendly, and I wasn't surprised, for a couple of reasons:

DUPLICITY

one, we were, after all, in New York. And two, she worked for a mob boss.

"I'm Harry Starke," I replied. "This is my associate, Heather Stillwell. Our appointment is for ten."

"Of course," she said. "Please take a seat. Mr. Massino will be with you in a few minutes."

"Thank you," Heather said, but the woman merely waved her hand and went back to her computer.

We did as she suggested and sat down together on one of the two black leather couches.

The office wasn't as luxurious as I'd expected, but then that wasn't too surprising either. *Maybe Massino likes to keep a low profile,* I thought. *Maybe an office on Wall Street is statement enough.*

It was almost twenty minutes later when the door at the far side of the room flew open and a tall, olive-skinned man walked toward us.

We stood up. He looked Heather up and down and then turned his attention to me.

"You must be Mr. Starke," he said but didn't offer me his hand.

"And you must be Mr. Massino," I said, not offering him mine. "This is my associate, Heather Stillwell."

"It's a pleasure to meet you both," he said dryly, his contempt obvious.

"If you'll follow me," he said, then turned and walked quickly back through the door from whence he'd come.

I glanced at Heather. She grinned at me. I nodded, and we followed him into a small hallway.

His office was... large, but not overly so. The wall to the right was all glass, floor to ceiling, and offered a stunning view of the street. The furniture was tasteful and obviously expensive. The two paintings on the wall to the left were originals, though I didn't know the artists. The carpet was Persian, and his desk was turn-of-the-century Roycroft.

"Please, take a seat," he said, gesturing to the two Stickley chairs in front of his desk. "You have fifteen minutes. What can I do for you?" he continued as he walked around the desk and sat down.

In the natural light of the windows, his dark hair was peppered with gray, and I estimated him to be in his late forties, maybe a little older.

He leaned back in the leather chair, steepled his fingers, and stared at me.

"We'd like to talk to you about Matteo Rossi," I said. "As I'm sure you know, he's missing; has been for more than a month. He was last seen leaving the Palace bar."

"Hmm..." Massino pursed his lips, thought for a moment, and then said, "I take it you're talking about that pigsty of a bar in Hell's Kitchen?"

I nodded. "It's owned by Romeo—"

"It's not owned by him," Massino said, cutting me off. "Necesaro owns the building, but he has nothing to do with the bar. Some guy named Frank something or other runs it for—"

"The Irish?" Heather asked, interrupting him.

He shrugged. "Maybe. Finn Doyle's people hang out there... But that's all I know. He and I have never quite seen eye to eye."

"But you know Rossi," I said.

He nodded. "I've known him since he was a child."

I locked eyes with him and waited, but he said nothing more.

"I hear Doyle and Rossi are close," I said, trying to get the conversation moving.

He nodded. "He is... or was. Doyle wants Matteo to join his little posse. Why, I don't know. The kid has little to offer..." He leaned forward a little and continued, "And Doyle's a man who will do whatever it takes to make it happen."

"Interesting..." I said. "And what about Matteo... and his family? We're having a hard time trying to figure out who he is. He's a total blank, no digital footprint."

Massino smiled. "That's because he doesn't want one, for whatever reason, and it makes him valuable... to some of us. As far as his family is concerned, Isabella Rossi is a special woman, albeit a little stubborn. We once were close, she and I."

So they were more than just friends.

"What do you think happened to Matteo?" I asked. "Is he dead? Is he in hiding? Or is he on the run?"

Again, he shrugged, then said, "Take your pick. Rossi was... is"—he corrected himself—"a law unto himself. Is he dead? I doubt it. He's not a smart man, but he's not stupid either. As to the other two options, that would depend on who he might have upset, in which case, my choice would be Finn Doyle. After all, he is the one who hired you. Is he not?"

Before I could answer, Heather cut in and said, "What about Catherine McCarthy, the mother of Matteo's son?"

His eyes darkened. "I know who she is and... what she is. I let her work here as my secretary for a few months, as a favor to Isabella. She's... loose. Not the kind of woman I want working for me."

"You mean..."

"I mean, the woman would sleep with anyone who could help her improve her station in life. She is a... whore."

Huh! She didn't strike me that way.

"When they were together?" Heather asked, frowning.

And again, he shrugged, turned the corners of his mouth down, scowling, and said, "I only know what I know from her time here. She and Matteo... Their relationship was... shaky. I don't usually waste my time worrying about such things, but again, I said, Isabella and I were... are, close. I consider her family, Catherine, too, so I take care of her."

Must be why she doesn't have to have a job, I thought.

"And Finn Doyle, how does he play into it?" I asked. "Why isn't Matteo working for you rather than him?"

"Isabella does not want her sons involved with me, and I respect her wishes. Finn Doyle? He is... *uomo cattivo*: a bad man. He is as vicious and conniving as his mother, Morrigan. Someone I know you also have experience with. Mr. Starke," he said and leaned forward. "I would be careful if I were you. He is not a man to be trifled with."

"He seemed genuinely concerned about him," Heather said.

"Of course he is," Massino said with a chuckle. "Everyone is always concerned about their hired men when something bad happens."

I narrowed my eyes. "So you think Doyle's concern is genuine?" I asked.

"Oh, Mr. Starke," he said, grinning wickedly. "Who can we say is genuine and who is not?"

I frowned. That wasn't the answer I was hoping for.

"Considering the circumstances, this may be a stupid question, Mr. Massino," I said. "Do you know of anyone who might want to... hurt Matteo?" I almost asked for his alibi for the night Matteo disappeared, but I knew it would be a waste of time. A man like Massino would never be caught without one.

He sighed and held up his hands as if in surrender. "It is indeed a stupid question, Mr. Starke, but I understand, and the answer is, there are many who would wish Matteo ill. It is the nature of the business we are in. But I will tell you this..." His smile faded. "I did not like the way Matteo was being treated. He could've been a valuable asset, given that he is a ghost, as they say. But he lives in a constant state of paranoia... and with good reason." Again, he shrugged and made a face. "However," he continued, "Finn Doyle is an imbecile. He wanted Matteo to prove himself, and that alone might have made him… want to run, perhaps. I think maybe Matteo wanted out."

"And leave his son?" Heather frowned and tilted her head in disbelief.

"Maybe you should pay Catherine a visit and meet the kid," Massino said, "and then you tell me what you think."

"You're saying he couldn't handle the baby?" Heather asked.

"Not everyone is cut out—" Massino was cut off by the ringing of his cell phone. He picked it up, glanced at the screen and said, "I'm sorry. I have to take this. I think I have given you enough of my time. Good luck to you, my friends."

What a frickin' waste of time, I thought savagely as I stood up. Massino had given us nothing but more rumors and hearsay.

"C'mon, Heather," I said. "Let's go."

16

"He knows more than he's telling," Heather said as we took the elevator to the ground floor. "I know he does, and he treated the meeting like it was a joke. He was sizing us up, Harry. Why would he want to do that?"

She was obviously just as frustrated as I was.

I texted George and told him to come and get us.

"I think we should go back in there," she said.

I shook my head. "No, we've wasted time on him. The problem with guys like him is that they know they have the upper hand. The only reason he agreed to see us was to size us up; see what he's dealing with. He thinks we're playing for the opposite team."

"Terrific," she groaned. "Now what?"

"I think we need to pay Isabella another visit, without Catherine present. There's something about their dynamic I don't like."

"And what about his comment about the kid?" Heather asked.

"Probably nothing to it," I replied.

"What if we are on the wrong team?" Heather asked quietly as George pulled up at the curb.

"We're on no one's team," I said. "We're neutral. It's our job to find the truth, no matter what. We can't let someone like Massino intimidate us. That's how they work. I don't play that way. He's obviously playing some sort of game with Doyle. We don't have to do that."

As I opened the door of the back passenger side for Heather, I froze, stunned.

"Top of the morning to ya both," Finn Doyle greeted us with a toothy smile that reminded me of a barracuda.

"Sorry, Harry. I had to let him in," George said. "He said he was your client."

"Ah, but he took a little persuadin', so he did," Doyle said, showing me a compact .380 revolver.

I grimaced. "Put that thing away, Doyle," I snapped, "or I'll take it away from you."

"Of course, ya will," he replied, bursting into a fit of laughter. He leaned sideways a little and shoved it into his pocket. "I was just trying to catch up with ya, me auld mate. I had a few of me guys to follow ya out of the Palace last night, but you seemed a little eager to get away, so ya did, rather than stay and chat, like."

I fought off the urge to land him one on his smug face. "Did you, now?" I said and gestured for Heather to get into the front seat while I took a seat next to our unwelcome visitor.

"What d'you want, Doyle?" I said as I sat down.

"I was just wantin' to know how the investigation is going, is all," he replied easily.

"It's not," I snapped. "Nobody's talking… well, they're talking, but they're not saying anything."

"Yeah, well then, and now you know how it was for me," Finn said, leaning his head back against the rest. "I thought I knew everything there was to know about him, but then he went and disappeared—and I don't t'ink he's in a dumpster somewhere. Not by anyone I know."

"What's your relationship like with Massino?" I asked.

"Ah, well now. Massino, you ask. He's nut'in' but an auld bastard, so he is," Finn said. "But here's the t'ing; just because we're not friends doesn't mean we're enemies, Mr. Starke. I know of his special relations with Isabella Rossi, and I wouldn't want to get in between that."

"What *are* their *relations*?" Heather turned in her seat to look at him. "That sounds... ominous."

"I don't know the details." Finn chuckled. "But I can assure you they're more than just friends."

"Well, that's good to know," I said, more sure than ever I needed to talk to Isabella Rossi alone. But I kept that to myself.

"Why don't we stop somewhere and get some lunch?" Heather said, giving me a look.

"That sounds good," I said and looked at Doyle. "Would you like to join us, Finn?"

He looked first at me, then at Heather, then at me again, then shook his head and said, "Well, now. It's a little early for me. I just wanted to make sure you wouldn't be swapping sides on me. Oh, and to remind you that I have eyes everywhere."

"Noted," I said easily. "I wouldn't have expected anything less."

"Good," he said, looking out the window. "You can drop me off right here. I have t'ings I need to get done."

George nodded and pulled over.

"Have a good day, Mr. Doyle," George said, turning in his seat to look at him.

"You as well," he said, grinning. Then he winked, hopped out, and closed the door with a bang.

I turned to look out the back window and watched as a black

sedan pulled up behind us, and with a wave, he climbed in beside the driver.

"Don't go yet, George," I said, watching the black car. "Wait till he's gone."

"He's a strange fellow," George said and chuckled as he pulled out into traffic.

"Did he really threaten you with his gun?" I asked. Strange was a good way to describe Finn Doyle, but I wasn't about to discuss him with my driver.

"He did." George rubbed his forehead. "And he gave me one hell of a fright."

"Sorry about that, George," I said. "I'll see you get a bonus for the... extra trouble. Now, I need you to take us back to the address on Shore Drive in Brooklyn."

"Sure thing," George said, his voice bright and cheery.

"You think we should stop somewhere and get some lunch? If he's having us watched..." Heather trailed off.

I shook my head. "I don't think so. He says he has eyes everywhere, and maybe he does, but screw him. He's not driving this investigation; we are."

"True," Heather said with a sigh. "I'll be glad when it's over."

I smiled and said, "I have a feeling we're just getting started, Heather."

The drive back to Brooklyn took almost forty-five minutes. We rode most of it in silence. I spent the time thinking, wondering if the wild goose chase was ever going to make any sense. *What the hell happened to Matteo Rossi? Is he dead... or what?*

"Here we are," George announced, pulling up outside the small house.

I stepped out of the car, noting the overcast skies. *An omen of dark things to come?* I wondered. It looked as if the clouds would open at any moment. I gritted my teeth, hoping it would hold off until we were back in the car.

"Maybe she'll be more welcoming this time," Heather said as she rang the doorbell. And then she rocked back and forth on her heels as we waited, and we waited.

"Ring it again," I said.

She nodded and pushed the button again. My phone buzzed in my pocket. I took it out and looked at the screen. It was Jacque.

As I took the call, the door opened. Isabella Rossi didn't look happy to see us.

"I have nothing to say to you," she said harshly, her nose in the air and her face stern. For a small woman, she certainly was feisty.

I nodded to Heather, then stepped away, leaving her to handle Isabella.

"Hey, Jacque, what's up?"

"We have a problem," Jacque said quickly. "You need to get out of the city ASAP."

"What?" I frowned. "Why? What's wrong?" I glanced back at Heather as she and Isabella disappeared into the house.

"Nothing's wrong," she said. "You need to go to Charleston, West Virginia, and you need to do it fast."

"Oh, come on, Jacque," I said. "Give."

"There's been a murder. Who and what, I don't know. I'm still trying to get the details, but they've put a BOLO out on Matteo Rossi."

I shook my head, trying to get a handle on what I was hearing. "Wait! What? How... how is he connected to a murder in West Virginia?"

"Sorry, Harry," she said. "I have no idea. I just know you and Heather need to get down there as soon as possible. All I can get out of the authorities there is that they found Rossi's driver's license at the scene."

"Then he must be on the run," I said, thinking hard. "We'll figure it out. Jacque, call Jerry and tell him to get the Gulfstream ready." I looked at my watch. "It's just after twelve now. We have to go back to the hotel and get our stuff, so... tell him one-thirty, or as close to it as we can make it."

"I'll do it," Jacque said. "In the meantime, I let the authorities in Charleston know you're coming."

17

Heather was still inside the house talking with Isabella Rossi, and I didn't want to miss out on the conversation, so I went inside and walked through to the living room just in time to hear Isabella say, "I don't know why he was so paranoid about the government. It was like I told you. His father dropped dead of a heart attack, and that was it. Matty swore it wasn't a heart attack—but it was. I know it was."

Heather was seated on the edge of an olive-colored velvet love seat; Isabella was in a wooden rocking chair.

"Why would he think that?" Heather asked.

"His father was an attorney." Isabella looked up at me as she spoke. She was still just as prickly as before, but there was a softness to her brown eyes. "He was working for the Massino family at the time, and he was only fifty-three. Matteo swore that Enzo was responsible and that he paid law enforcement to cover it up and say it was a heart attack. But... I don't think so." She heaved a heavy sigh. "My late husband's father died of a heart attack when he was forty-nine, and his father before him. It's their genes; that and a bad diet."

I nodded. "You're probably right," I said. "But speaking of Massino." I narrowed my eyes and looked at her. "What exactly is your relationship with him?"

She pressed her lips tightly together, breathed deeply, then said, "It's complicated. I've known Enzo since I was a girl. He was there for me when my husband Niccolo passed away. It was always platonic until... I don't know when it changed."

Aha. That's what I thought.

"So you and Enzo were lovers?" Heather asked.

She shrugged. "For a short while. Nicci was gone and I was killing myself trying to keep this place going, never leaving and barely getting by. Enzo stepped in and helped tie up the loose ends. He was good to me." She shrugged again and continued, "It didn't last long. He soon tired of me. But we remained friends until..."

"Until what?" I asked.

"Until Matty got himself involved with Finn Doyle's people."

"So, he wasn't happy about your son being involved with the Irish?" Heather asked.

Isabella shook her head. "No, he wasn't, but he had nothing to do with what happened to Matteo. None of us do. I thought *he* would've hired a private detective, not Finn."

"Why didn't he then?" I asked.

Maybe it's because he doesn't want him found, I thought.

Isabella seemed to be trying not to roll her eyes at me. "I don't know," she said. "I don't ask him for favors like that, and..." She paused, took a deep breath, and said, "Look, he has people out there looking for him, too. Some of them better than private detectives."

"Fair enough," I said, smiling, not taking offense. Truth be told, she was probably right.

"Why didn't you want to talk in front of Catherine?" I asked.

"I wasn't in the mood." She waved a hand as if to shoo the question away, and by the look on her face, I knew she was lying.

She looked at me, and I could tell she knew what I was thinking. She shook her head, then said, "She's a fine woman… Maybe a little loose, but…"

Maybe it has something to do with Massino, I thought. After all, he had mentioned that Catherine had worked for him, and if Isabella was *with* Massino at the time… Well, I could see how that could cause tension. And with Catherine hooked up with Matteo. *What a frickin' mess.*

My phone buzzed in my pocket. I took it out, glanced at the screen, and saw I had a text from George reminding me we needed to get moving.

"Is there anything else you can tell us, Mrs. Rossi?" I asked, ignoring the strange look from Heather. She didn't know about the murder in West Virginia and the connection to Matteo, and I wasn't about to tell Isabella. Though I *did* need to know if he had any friends there.

"He was an upstanding young man," Isabella replied, pushing her chest out. "He wasn't like his brother. He's never gotten into trouble. And he hasn't gotten in touch with me, not since that night, which is why I know something bad must've happened to him."

"Does he have any friends in West Virginia?" I asked, again ignoring the questioning look from Heather.

Isabella raised her eyebrows. "No, not at all. I doubt he's ever been there. Why do you ask?"

"It was just a thought," I said. "If you think of anything else, please let us know." I handed her my card. "That has my cell number on it. Call me anytime. Now, we've taken up enough of your time. Thank you, Isabella."

She nodded. "I hope you find him, but I don't think you will."

It was a cryptic response, but I didn't have time to sit and pick it apart. "Heather?" I said, then turned and headed for the door.

"What in the world?" Heather demanded as we slid into the back of the SUV. "West Virginia? And what's the hurry? She was just beginning to open up."

"We have to go to West Virginia," I said and then explained what had happened and what I'd learned from Jacque.

"Wow," Heather muttered. "So do we know who the victim is?"

"Not yet," I replied. "I'm still waiting for the details. We're going in blind."

"Well, this'll be fun," Heather said dryly.

George shuttled us back to the hotel, where we quickly packed and checked out.

"Geez, what a rush," Heather said as we loaded the bags into the car. "I'm hungry. D'you think we'll have lunch on the plane?"

"Might not be much," I said as George pulled out onto the street and headed for the airport. "But there's usually something to eat."

We rode in silence for the next several miles, and then Heather looked at me and said, "D'you think someone could've planted his driver's license at the scene to throw us off?"

It was a question I'd been asking myself.

"Experience tells me that's exactly what happened," I replied. "What're the odds of a driver's license being dropped at a crime scene? If that's what happened, it would be a first."

"I've never come across anything like it either," she said.

"And given that Matteo has gone to great lengths to conceal himself, it seems out of character."

"It would be if he's still alive," I said. "But if he's dead, it would make perfect sense for the killer to dump the license. It would send the authorities off on a wild goose chase like no other."

She shook her head, seemingly lost in thought, then said, "What a twisted web we have, and it's getting worse." She leaned her head back and closed her eyes.

"That it is," I agreed. And I, too, closed my eyes, wondering what the next several hours held for us.

By two o'clock in the afternoon, we were wheels up into a clear blue sky. The crew supplied sandwiches and coffee for lunch, and we'd barely finished eating when Jerry announced we were on our final approach into Charleston. I still hadn't heard from Jacque, but I was able to send Amanda a text to update her and tell her I hoped we'd be home soon. And then, as we descended through the thin cloud cover, I tried to figure out what my approach to the authorities on the ground would be. *Geez, I hate going blind into a crime scene.*

What made things worse was that I didn't have any connections in West Virginia, so there was no telling what kind of treatment Heather and I would receive from the PD. And who could blame them? I knew from personal experience that private investigators can be a real pain in the ass. All I could do was hope for the best. Matteo Rossi didn't have a missing person's report out for him, and so *maybe* they'd believe he was missing, and *maybe* they wouldn't. There was no telling.

We landed in Charleston, West Virginia, at three-ten that afternoon, and as soon as the wheels hit the Tarmac, Heather and I were on the move. Jacque, bless her, had arranged a rental, so after directing Jerry to find him and his crew a hotel room for

DUPLICITY

the night, we said our thanks and goodbyes, grabbed our luggage and piled it into the back of yet another black SUV.

"Where to first?" Heather asked as she climbed into the driver's seat.

I plugged in the coordinates and said, "The police department first, then, hopefully, the crime scene."

18

It was just after three-forty-five when we arrived at the Charleston Police Department on Court Street that afternoon. We parked out front, fed the meter, stood for a moment, then mounted the four shallow steps and pushed through the front doors.

"Good afternoon," the woman at the front desk greeted us brightly. "You must be Harry and Heather?"

I looked at her in surprise, then said, "Yes, that's us."

"Perfect," she said. "I'll let Chief Wilbur know you're here. He's been expecting you. He's been talking to your partner, Jacque, I believe? So, if you'll take a seat…"

I nodded. "Thank you."

Heather and I exchanged glances and stepped back to wait while she made the call. I couldn't hear what she was saying, but she was upbeat and smiling, and that in itself was a win.

"If you'll follow me," she said, stepping out from behind her desk, "I'll show you to his office."

"Here you go," she said, pushing open a heavy oak door. "Go on in. He's waiting for you."

"Thank you," I said, and she smiled, nodded, and then turned and headed back down the corridor.

We stepped through the door into a large, dark, dated room where Chief Wilbur was seated behind a cluttered desk, his bald head shining beneath the aging fluorescent lights. He had that stereotypical chief appearance: meticulously pressed blue uniform with four stars on each collar, gruff, a little stout, and aged somewhere in his mid to late forties.

"Mr. Starke. Miss Stillwell. Good afternoon," he greeted us as he stood and smiled at us over a pair of round wire-rimmed reading glasses. He offered his hand. We both shook it, and then he said, "I hope you had a good flight. You were in a bit of a rush, so I'm told. Nice lady, that Jacque Hale. Your business partner, so I understand. She sounds efficient. Good job, good job. Now, you're here about the murder at the Ford dealership?"

"We are," I said, making the assumption that the dealership was the crime scene. "I understand you found Matteo Rossi's driver's license at the scene."

The chief nodded, sucked on his bottom lip, then said, "Yes, that's true. But it's more complicated than that, I'm afraid. What do you know about Rossi?"

"Not much," I said. "He's managed to stay under the radar for most of his adult life. No bank accounts, credit cards, or traceable cell phones. Just a social security number and... the driver's license. My IT guy is still working on it, but so far, the man seems to be something of a ghost, and he's been missing for more than a month. That's how we're involved. We've been hired to find him."

Chief Wilbur removed his reading glasses and set them on the desk. "That's what we've been running into. Do you happen to have a current photo of him? His driver's license was issued four years ago, and the photo is... well, it's a DMV photo, and you know how that goes," he said with a grin.

Heather reached into her pocket and retrieved the photograph Finn Doyle had supplied. She glanced at the back, then handed it to him. "This one was taken eight months ago."

He looked at it, shook his head, and said, "This guy doesn't look anything like the man caught by the security camera or what the witness described."

"There was a witness?" I asked, thinking that maybe things were beginning to move in the right direction. "How did he describe the perp?"

"The witness is a she," Wilbur said. "She described a light-complected man with blond hair," Wilbur continued, staring at the photo. "D'you mind if I have a copy made of this?" He looked up at me. I nodded. "Thank you. No, this isn't a match. I don't think this is the same person. Though I suppose he could have dyed his hair…"

I didn't like the way my gut was knotting up. Something about it wasn't sitting right with me.

"Would you mind telling us what happened?" I asked politely.

"Well, based on the witness account and the security footage," Wilbur began, "we know that Dahlia Winters showed up for work around eight-thirty this morning. She heard a commotion coming from one of the back rooms, and at first, she didn't think much about it. Greg Mallen, the owner, is usually there before she is and, apparently, is a bit of a tyrant; he shouts a lot. Anyway, after a couple of minutes, she heard a loud pop and went to investigate. When Dahlia made it to the back office, where the keys to the vehicles are stored, she saw a blond-haired man run out and into the parking lot. She didn't see anything but the back of his head. However, the security camera in the hallway also caught him, and from the same angle—his back—so unfortunately we don't have a facial.

"Dahlia found Greg Mallen lying face down on the floor.

He'd been shot once in the back of the head. CSI found Rossi's driver's license under the desk. And that's about all we have so far. I was hoping you could fill in some of the blanks."

I ignored that for the moment and said, "I'm guessing he stole a car, right?"

"He did, a 2020 white Chevy Blazer," Wilbur said. "He tossed the license plate. My guys found it in the parking lot. So my guess is he put another plate on it."

"Terrific," I muttered. "That'll make it damn near impossible to find."

"It will," he replied. "Which is why I was hoping you'd be able to give me more information on Matteo Rossi. We ran his name, but nothing came up. And there's not a missing person's report, so when your office called, I was surprised, to say the least."

"It's a complicated case," I said. "We're still trying to figure it out. His folks didn't want to file a report. His mother's convinced he's dead, but I'm not so sure. No one wants to talk."

"Yes, well," Wilbur said, "I'm thinking maybe there were two men involved. Rossi could've been waiting outside."

"Wouldn't the cameras have picked that up?" I asked. "And if that's true, how did Rossi's license get inside the office?"

"The exterior cameras weren't working. Maintenance was scheduled to work on them tomorrow. According to Dahlia Winters, Mallen wasn't concerned because they don't have a lot of problems there. The exterior cameras had been down for more than a week, which surprised me considering the dealership is right off Interstate 64, so I wasn't surprised a car was stolen. Had it not been for the driver's license, I would have put it down as a crime of convenience. With Mallen being in the wrong place at the wrong time."

"Were there any signs of a struggle?" I asked.

"Some," he replied, "but nothing big. CSI is still working

the scene, but from what I saw, the place was fairly clean. There were powder burns on the back of his head, so it looks like an execution. He must have gotten a good look at the guy."

I nodded. But the placement of the driver's license didn't make any sense. It was obviously planted, which, as far as I was concerned, meant little; it wasn't helpful. If Rossi was dead, I figured it had been planted to throw us off the trail. If he was alive—and my gut was telling me he was—then someone was obviously trying to frame him for Mallen's murder. Or... none of the above.

"Do you have pictures of the driver's license?" I asked.

He nodded. "It's been bagged and tagged, so the photos should be in the system by now. Lemme take a look."

He shifted around in his seat to face his computer.

"Yup! Here we go."

He turned the monitor around so we could see it.

The photo was a closeup of the front and back of the license. It was Matteo Rossi's active driver's license, all right. Matteo looked much like he did in our photo, only a little younger, and he wasn't smiling.

"And here it is in relation to the body." Wilbur clicked the arrow to take us to the next photo. It showed the license lying about two feet from Mallen's head and just underneath the front of the desk, in line of sight. In fact, it stood out like a sore thumb on the dark gray tile.

"It almost looks..." Heather didn't finish her thought; she didn't have to. I agreed with her. I wasn't sure that Rossi had been there at all. We already knew he wasn't the blond man Dahlia Winters had described and who'd been caught on the internal camera.

"I don't have the footage yet," Wilbur said as he flipped to the next photo. It was a closeup of Greg Mallen's body lying face down, blood soaking his gray hair. He was wearing a white dress shirt, black pants, and black dress shoes. His arms were splayed out in front of him. I figured the blast from the gun had thrown him forward.

And Wilbur was right. The next photo was a wide view of the office. Nothing looked disturbed, but again, the license was visible under the front of the desk.

I don't get it, I thought. *It makes no sense. There's no way Rossi could have dropped it there. It's in the wrong place. The blond guy must have placed it there and made sure it was easily seen. But we know it wasn't him, so it means nothing. Hmm. Is it possible Matteo dyed his hair? If he did, it doesn't explain the guy's lighter complexion. Then again, people see what they see, and from the grainy security footage... It's difficult to tell.*

"What do you think, Mr. Starke?" Wilbur asked, leaning back in his chair, smiling. "You appear to be stumped."

I shrugged, nodded, and said, "Yup. It doesn't make sense, does it?"

"It sure doesn't," he replied. "So what are you thinking?"

"I'm thinking I'd like to take a look at the crime scene, if that's okay with you."

He nodded. "I'll get you some passes. The witness was there as of about thirty minutes ago, and she might still be there. You can chat with her, too. I don't mind the extra set of hands. I'm just a hair disappointed you didn't have more to give me on Rossi."

"Me, too," I agreed. *Me, too.*

19

We left Wilbur at his desk and returned to the car. As I started the engine, I glanced at Heather. She pursed her lips and shook her head.

"What?" I asked.

"You're thinking the same as me. You don't think it was Rossi either, do you? I'm also thinking we should call Doyle. After all, he *is* the one footing the bill."

"Let's get something to eat first," I said. "We can hit a drive-through on the way there."

"Okay," she said, leaning her head back against the rest and closing her eyes. "But you know we're on a wild goose chase, Harry, and I don't like it at all."

I nodded but said nothing as I followed the GPS toward the dealership. It was, as Wilbur said, situated right off the interstate.

It was, by then, almost five-thirty. The interview with Wilbur had lasted longer than I'd expected.

We hit the McDonald's drive-through on East Washington and ordered McNuggets and coffee, a snack to tide us over until we had time for dinner. The dealership was just a few blocks away, so we sat for a moment in the parking lot to eat.

"You're right," I said. "I don't know where this is taking us, but I don't know that we're in the wrong place."

"What do you mean?" Heather asked.

"Well. Think about it," I said, then took a sip of my coffee before continuing. "If the guy who killed Mallen planted Rossi's license, where did he get it from? Either he took it from him, or someone gave it to him. Either way, it's a link to Rossi."

She shot me a weary look. "Yeah, but for all we know, the guy could've picked it up off the sidewalk."

"True," I conceded. "But at this point, it's all we have."

She laughed and shook her head.

"Time to go take a look," I said, then changed my mind. "No, I need to give Jacque a call first."

I made the call and put the phone on speaker so Heather could listen in.

"I take it the two of you made it, then?" Jacque said.

"Alive and well," I replied. "We're at a McDonald's near the scene of the crime. What have you got for us?"

"Let me bring Tim in," she replied. "Give me a sec."

We waited in silence, taking advantage of the time to eat, until Jacque got on the line with Tim.

"Hey, Harry. It's me," Tim said. "How's it going?"

"Not good," I replied. "I need you to look into Greg Mallen. He's the victim, shot once in the head execution style at the car dealership he owns. Mallen New and Used Cars."

"Okay, okay," Tim hummed. "I'll start digging right now."

I nodded and then proceeded to brief them on what we had learned so far, which wasn't much. I finished up and then waited for someone to say something.

"You there?" Heather asked, frowning.

"Yes," Jacque said. "I'm just a little lost for words. Why West Virginia?"

"I don't know," I said. "I asked Isabella Rossi, but she said as far as she knew, Matteo had never been to West Virginia. That, though, may or may not be true."

"It looks like Mallen lived all his life in Charleston," Tim said. "His grandfather opened the dealership back in the forties, and then from there, it was passed down through the generations to Greg. His son, Colby, is next in line to take over the family business."

"Could he have lived in New York at any time?" Heather asked.

"I don't think so," Tim replied. "He may have traveled there, but other than that… he appears to be clean."

"Crime of opportunity, then?" Jacque said. "What about the driver's license?"

"I think it was planted," Heather said. "I can't see Greg Mallen asking to see the man's license if he was being held at gunpoint."

I gave Heather a wry look and shook my head.

"Could it have been Matteo?" Jacque asked. "He could have bleached his hair."

"Could have," I said, "though I don't think so. And, from what I've heard, I don't think he's a killer, either. A chronic paranoid? Maybe, but not a killer.

"Maybe he's mentally disturbed," Heather said. "That could be a driving factor. He could be on the run. Maybe in some sort of delusional state."

"I wonder if he's ever been hospitalized," I said.

"Nope," Tim answered. "Not that I can find. There are no medical records unless he was admitted under an alias."

"Which everyone says that he didn't use," Heather said.

"Did the video include the room where the struggle took place?" Jacque asked.

"No," I replied. "Just the hallway."

"It's been a *long* day," Heather muttered, eyeing me. "Don't you think it's time we got over there?"

"I find it a little strange," Tim said, "that the moment you guys start looking for Matteo, a big lead pops up, like a license being found at the scene of a murder. If the license was planted, it makes sense it was planted to throw you off."

"If it wasn't for the license, we wouldn't be in West Virginia. It was planted to bring us here. The question is, why? I have a feeling it could have nothing to do with Rossi. As far as we know, no one in Rossi's circle has ties to Charleston. And, according to Chief Wilbur, there's not a lot of mob activity here either."

"But the dealership is right next to a major highway," Heather said. "Someone passing through… in need of a car. A crime of opportunity—"

"We're talking in circles," I said, cutting her off. "We need to go, get eyes on the place. We might be sitting on a mine of information and not even know."

I know I sounded irritated, and I was. We were going round and round beating a dead horse, and it was getting us nowhere.

"Well, don't let us keep you then," Jacque said. "Go see what you can find out. In the meantime, we'll keep beating the bushes."

"Talk to you later," I said and hung up.

I looked at Heather and shook my head. "That was a waste of thirty minutes," I said.

"That's hard, Harry," she said.

"Maybe," I said. "Maybe it's me. I have a headache starting to bother me. But let's go do this."

20

THE DEALERSHIP WAS A HIVE OF ACTIVITY. THERE MUST HAVE been a dozen police cruisers parked on the road, along with two fire trucks and a huge, black CSI rapid response vehicle.

It was, of course, taped off. We walked the perimeter and flashed our passes to one of the uniformed officers out front. He nodded, lifted the tape to allow us to enter, and we walked past a row of brand-new Ford SUVs to the showroom.

We stepped inside and walked across to the reception area, where two plain-clothed detectives were talking together. I smiled to myself at the picture they made. I'd seen it all so many times before, the stereotypical detective partnership. One older, gray-haired short and tubby man; the other much younger, brown hair, tall and thin.

"You must be Mr. Starke, the infamous PI we've been hearing about all day. I'm Ted Williams," the older man said, sticking out his hand. "Chief Wilbur said you'd be showing up soon. This is Detective Harris, my rookie partner."

Infamous? I wasn't sure if he was being sarcastic or not, so I ignored it, shook his hand and said, "Harry Starke. This is my associate, Heather Stillwell."

"Harry..." he said. "Is it all right if I call you Harry?"

I nodded. He nodded, and his mood seemed to lighten.

"The chief said you've been briefed on what happened here this morning."

"That's right," I replied. "Anything new?"

He shook his head. "Nope. CSI's just finishing up. It's pretty clean. You heard about the DL, right? What, exactly, is your connection, Harry?"

I knew that was coming, so I quickly filled them in on what we were doing—a condensed version—and what we'd learned so far. Condensed or not, it took a good five minutes, and I was getting more antsy by the moment.

"...I understand there's security footage. Can we see it?" I finished. "And I'd like to have a copy sent to my IT guy for analysis, if possible."

"I think that can be arranged," Williams said, thrusting his hands into his pants pockets. "Right now, CSI has everything locked down, as you can see." He cast a glance around the showroom, as did I.

There was a Mustang GT at one end and a Chevy Camaro at the other. Strange to see two such rivals parked in the same dealership, but what did I know?

"This killing is going to upset a lot of people," he continued. "Greg Mallen was a nice fella and an upstanding member of the community, as is his family, and he was well loved by everyone. It makes no sense."

It was, indeed, senseless, but most murders never do make sense.

I nodded along anyway, taking in the perfectly landscaped flowerbeds outside of the main entrance. From the lack of an ambulance, I figured Greg Mallen's body was long gone on its way to the medical examiner. I was, however, less interested in that than I was in figuring out if Rossi had actually been there.

My gut was telling me he was still alive, but was he? I had to believe he was. My gut feelings had rarely let me down, and I had a strong feeling they weren't going to this time. But if he was alive, what the hell was he up to? Why was he on the run, and why hadn't he contacted his family? And, more to the point, where was he going? If he had been there at the dealership, he was obviously heading south.

"Is your witness still here?" I asked.

"No," Harris said. "She went home about thirty minutes ago. She's... a little frazzled, to say the least."

"She's a reliable witness, though," Williams added. "She called it in as soon as she found him. The perp was still here; he ran past her in the hallway. I'm surprised he didn't turn on her. She says that she caught a glimpse of his face as he ran past her."

"Really?" I said, my hopes rising a little. I needed to talk to this woman and show her the picture of Rossi.

"Was she able to describe him?" Heather asked as we followed the two detectives back toward the offices.

"Here, put these on," Williams said, handing us each a pair of latex gloves.

"She said he was of average height and had blond hair and startling blue eyes. That's all she was able to see. She only saw him for a second," Harris said.

"Rossi has dark hair," Heather said. "And brown eyes."

"He could've used a disguise, though, right?" Williams said as we approached what I assumed was Mallen's office.

"He could," I said, not knowing what else to say. We'd already beaten it to death ad nauseam, and I was in no mood to continue it.

"This is it," Williams said as he pointed to the taped-off door. "This is where Dahlia Winters found him. There's a door at the end of the hallway"—he pointed—"that opens out onto the rear parking area. This office is where they keep the keys. It's also the employee entrance."

"Is that the way your witness came in?" I asked.

He nodded. "That's when she saw our guy. As I said, he ran past her. The footage shows him running from the office to the back entrance just as she entered. See?" He pointed to a camera over the door through which we'd just entered the hallway.

"Pretty cut and dried, if you ask me," Harris said.

"Nobody's asking you," Williams said, then continued, "Sure, we don't have footage of him actually committing the murder, but he was in here less than a minute after Mallen. You're an ex-cop. You know how it works."

"How d'you know I'm an ex-cop?" I asked.

"I googled you, for Pete's sake. The chief told me who you were; said it was okay for me to talk to you. But we ain't the country hicks most folk think we are. I don't talk to nobody I don't feel good about. But I figured I might learn something, so here we are."

I looked again at the security camera. If the perp had come in the back way, he should have been looking straight toward the camera.

"I know what you're thinking," Williams said. "I thought that, too. I figured we'd for sure have this guy on the camera. And we do, but he had his hood up and he kept his head down."

"Makes sense," I said. "If he's been around the block, he would assume there would be cameras, especially at the entrances and exits."

"But what about the ones on the outside of the building?" Harris asked. "We know they're not working, but he didn't, and he would have been dodging and ducking those."

"I'm sure he was," I replied. "Did your witness say if he was alone or if there was someone else in the car with him?"

"I asked that," Williams said. "She said she didn't notice. And she wouldn't have. She didn't know anything was wrong."

I nodded. "We don't know what he was doing out there, and I'm assuming you haven't found another car, so we don't know how he got here. He either walked, had a partner who drove the other car away and dumped it, or someone dropped him off... Hell, he might have even taken an Uber."

Detective Williams grimaced. "Damn cameras." He pointed down the hall to the clouded glass door where a tech was dusting for fingerprints. "That's the entrance and exit door. From the footage, we know the perp followed Mallen in forty-seven seconds after he arrived. Mallen appeared to be unaware he was being followed."

"Is this an automatic locking door?" Heather asked.

He shook his head. "Mallen unlocked it and then stepped in. He opened the door and walked in, head down. Then he paused. Then he walked slowly along the corridor to this here office and stepped inside; the door was wide open. He was in there for three minutes fifty-five seconds. Then the guy ran out through the back door."

I nodded, thinking that it sounded as if the perp didn't know the layout of the dealership, furthering the theory that it was a crime of opportunity, making it all the more possible that it *was* Rossi.

"You can take a look," Williams said, nodding to the open door.

He stepped inside. I followed, so did Heather; Harris stayed just outside the door.

The body was gone, but I was familiar with the scene from looking at the stills in Wilbur's office. There was a yellow marker where the driver's license had been, but there was little else to see.

"Williams," a stern female voice cut in. "Give my people some room to breathe."

I glanced at the thin, middle-aged, dark-haired woman, dressed head to toe in white Tyvek coveralls and pegged her as the CSI supervisor.

"This is the PI that Chief Wilbur told us about," Williams said. "I was just giving him the rundown."

"Right," she snapped, her blue eyes shooting daggers at Heather and me. "Well, I'm sure you can respect the fact that I'm trying to finish up here. It's bad enough that the media have been standing around outside for hours. Now I have this to deal with."

"I know, I know, Helen." Wiliams' tone lightened, and it was easy to see which of the two held the authority in their working relationship. "I was hoping you could tell them what you've found."

He turned to us and said, "This is Helen Cortez, our CSI supervisor. Helen, this is Harry Starke and his partner Heather."

"We've found a driver's license," she began, before we could say anything. "Minor blood splatter from a well-aimed shot to the back of the head. Security footage that's grainy at best. Missing keys for a newer model white Chevy Blazer. That's about it. I'm hoping the forensics will provide us with some sort of lead."

She was a brusque and obviously competent woman, not one to waste time on the niceties.

"What about the driver's license?" I asked. "Is it legitimate?"

She pursed her lips, then said, "It's a standard New York state license. Yes, it's legit, though the photo didn't match what little we could see of the man in the security footage. Best case scenario, the fellow in the footage disguised himself. Worst case, he took the license from someone during a robbery, then he killed the guy. We found the Chevy's dealer tag out in the lot. My guess is this is a random crime, and the perp planted the license to throw us off. Truth be told, the guy is out of state by now, and if he's smart enough to have changed the plates, we'll have the devil of a job finding him. Might never find him, not unless we get lucky and find a DNA match."

"And hopefully, you will," I said, eyeing the blood stain on the office floor. It had already congealed, a deep black stain peppered with crimson. "Is there any way I could get a look at the footage before we go?"

Helen Cortez pursed her lips, annoyance written all over her face. "It's been sent off for analysis, but I'll grab my laptop and pull the file up for you. But not here. We can do it in the showroom."

I nodded. "Thank you, Helen. I really appreciate it."

"You're welcome," she said wryly.

I glanced once more around the office, my gaze lingering for a moment on the yellow marker, the spot where they found the license. From the doorway, it was in plain sight. And once again, something just didn't feel right about it.

21

Helen set her laptop down on the Parts counter and opened it. She flipped through several screens, selected a folder, opened it, and then stood back a little so we could all see.

"As you can see," she said, "it's grainy, and I don't expect we'll get much from it. But here you go." She tapped, and the time stamp at the bottom right-hand corner began to move.

For several moments, all we could see was the hallway. Then the door at the far end opened and a man I assumed was Greg Mallen walked in, closing the door behind him. Helen was right; the image was incredibly grainy. It was impossible to tell his mood, if Mallen was distressed or not, but from the way he walked leisurely into the office, flipped on the lights and closed the door behind him, he appeared to be fine.

I watched the time stamp carefully. Forty-seven seconds later, a hooded figure came through the door. He entered, wearing what looked like a dark sweatshirt and jeans. He seemed to be wandering along the hallway as if he was looking for something. Never once did he look up. He looked at one door, then another, trying the knob on each as he went. My guess was he'd never been inside the building before and had no idea what he was walking into.

The man passed by the first office on the left and the one on the right, then stopped in front of the door through which Mallen had just disappeared and stared at it.

A couple of seconds more, and he reached out, grasped the knob, turned it, walked into the office, closing the door behind him.

I looked at the time stamp, waiting.

Two minutes twelve seconds later, there was a flash of light through the glass. And one minute forty-three seconds later, the door was flung open, and the hooded figure ran out, leaving the door wide open, the hood now off his head, revealing a shock of dirty blond hair. The whole thing had taken exactly three minutes fifty-five seconds.

Oh, yes. He's the killer, all right.

"Can you stop the tape and run it back a little—to where he comes out the door? There! Yes, that's good... Nope. Can't see his face. You can continue."

The man ran to the door, but just before he reached it, it opened, and a woman stepped inside. He hesitated, just for a second, then shoved past her and ran outside. She turned, looked after him, shook her head and then proceeded along the hallway. Then she turned, looked out, and closed the door. I figured she must have gotten at least a quick look at his face. We watched her enter the office, and then Helen stopped the video.

"That's it," she said. "Not much there, is there?"

"Hmm," Heather said. "He doesn't look much like the Rossi in our photo. And the video..."

"Yes," Helen said. "It's an old, worn-out system. Should have been replaced years ago. Having said that, my guess is it's not the guy on the driver's license. This man had a shade of hair that would not be easily achieved for a man who had nearly black hair only a month ago."

I nodded. "I agree. His hair would be a brighter, more yellow blond, rather than the natural shade we saw in the video." I paused for a minute, then continued, "I think there must have been someone waiting outside for him. That would explain the change of license plates. With the hurry he was in, he wouldn't have bothered otherwise, which would also explain how he got here; there was a second vehicle."

"We haven't found any evidence of that," Helen said. "All we found was the dealer plate lying on the ground. It was held on by bungies. But that doesn't mean anything. We'll have a bullet, of course, but there was no casing, so I figure it was probably a small caliber revolver, a thirty-two, perhaps. He was wearing gloves, so no prints. Maybe the hair and fiber people will be able to find enough to lift some DNA. If not…" She trailed off and shook her head.

"I still think it was someone passing through," Detective Williams said. "It's the only thing that makes any sense. The more I watch the video, the more I think the suspect didn't know what he was doing."

"You may be right," I said. "If so, the only way to explain the license is that the perp is somehow connected to my case, to Matteo Rossi. As to him not knowing what he was doing, he pulled the trigger on George Mallen pretty damn quick. There might have been a struggle, but it didn't look likely to me. It sure as hell didn't take the suspect long to decide that murder was the option."

"Well, it wouldn't, would it?" Heather said, looking at me. "Not if he's a killer. Harry, have you thought that the guy might be on a mission, same as us? Maybe the killer is looking for him, too. That would explain the license, wouldn't it?"

I looked at her, furrowed my brows, and said, nodding, "Could be. That would explain a lot."

"I agree," Helen said, snapping the laptop shut. "I'll have the footage sent to your office. D'you have a card?"

I handed her one, thanked her, and she turned away and left, presumably back to the office. Then I turned to the two detectives.

"So, d'you have an address for the witness? I'd like to show her the more recent photo of Rossi and see what she thinks, though I'm pretty sure I know the answer."

Williams nodded, took out his phone, scrolled through several screens, then texted the address and phone number to me.

"She was pretty shaken up when she left. I'm sharing my notes with you, Harry, just in case you find something we didn't. Sometimes people remember things, don't they?"

I nodded. "We'll see what we can do, but I can't make any promises. We haven't had a lot of luck so far. This is a... It's a strange one: Lots of questions, few answers, and the answers we do have may not all be true."

Williams chuckled. "I think just about every case I get is strange. It's the job, as I'm sure you know."

"I do," I replied, then thanked them both for their time. Cops rarely allow private investigators into their confidence, much less an active crime scene, and I appreciated it. And I wished I could have been more help to them.

"It wasn't Rossi," Heather stated with conviction as we climbed into the SUV. "What do you think?"

"I agree," I replied as I started the engine and then punched in the coordinates of Dahlia Winters' home. "No matter, we have to talk to the witness. We don't know what was going on outside of the dealership. Rossi could have been there waiting for him. What bugs me, though, is the driver's license. The perp must have planted it. Where did he get it? More to the point, *how* did he get it? Geez, the only thing we know for sure is that Rossi doesn't have it with him."

I chuckled and glanced at her. She was smiling.

Dahlia Winters lived two miles east of the dealership, tucked away in a small, quaint neighborhood made up of older houses. It was the kind of place that once was a quiet little suburb, but as the city grew around it, it became surrounded by industrial estates.

Dahlia's home was a mid-size ranch, probably built in the mid-seventies. It was obviously loved by its owner: freshly painted white with black accents, and she'd obviously spent a lot on curb appeal. The lawns were neatly trimmed, and at least two dozen hydrangeas surrounded the front porch.

I pulled into the driveway, noting chalk art on the blacktop, and I assumed there must be a child in the home. And, for a moment, the sight of it made me miss my Jade, but I pushed it away. I always missed Jade—and Amanda—when I was out of town, and it never did the investigation any good for me to dwell on it.

We mounted the four steps to the screened porch and stepped up to the front door. There was no doorbell, so I knocked on the door and then took a couple of steps back. And we waited.

"Maybe she's not home?" Heather said, turning to glance back toward the SUV and then at the garage door.

I nodded, waited another minute, then knocked again.

A moment later, the door opened and we were confronted by a short, red-haired woman wearing a white, terry-cloth robe.

"I'm so sorry," she said. "I was in the shower. Can I help you with something?"

22

"Sorry for the mess," Dahlia Winters said as she led us through to her living room, dodging the toddler toys in the foyer. "I'm usually at work until six, and my mom watches my daughter. My husband won't be home until seven, so I thought I had some time to clean up."

"You're fine," I said, smiling.

I figured she was in her mid-twenties and that the red hair probably came out of a bottle.

She looked at me. She looked exhausted, and I couldn't help but feel sorry for her. She'd obviously been traumatized by what had happened at the dealership.

The living room was a conglomeration of mismatched furniture, clean but cluttered. "You all can sit wherever you'd like. Are you thirsty? Coffee, tea, or water?"

I smiled at her. "I'm fine, thank you. I think you've probably had enough coffee for one day."

"I'm going to get dressed. I'll be right back," she said. Heather and I waited patiently. We both checked our phones for any updates from Jacque and Tim. Nothing.

She returned and took a seat across from us on a long, plaid-covered couch. She glanced around, sighed, then said, "I'm sorry. It's a mess, isn't it? We're getting new furniture next month. It all takes time. We're trying to pay off our credit cards…" She shrugged and clasped her hands together in front of her.

"Your home is lovely," Heather said. "There's absolutely nothing to apologize for. I still have my grandmother's couch from the seventies in my living room. It doesn't match anything, and I don't care."

Dahlia nodded, visibly relaxed, and smiled at her.

"So you're private detectives?" she said. "Did the Mallen family hire you? I was kind of thinking that they might do something like that. They don't like the police department here."

"Really?" I said, frowning. "Why's that? Do they have history with them?"

"No, I don't think so." She shook her head, wrapping her arms around her faded blue T-shirt. She was a petite woman and could easily have passed for a teenager. She shifted a little, then pulled her feet up onto the couch and wrapped her arms around her knees.

"Then what?" I asked, trying not to sound too forceful with this woman, who was clearly shaken up.

She shrugged. "I don't know a lot about the Mallen family. I've worked there for about five years now, but they're a tight-knit family. They don't let just anyone into their inner circle—and I definitely didn't make the cut. I'm not from around here, you know. We only moved to Charleston to make it easier for Drew and me to get work. We're planning to get out of the city as soon as we can."

I nodded. "But how do you know they don't like the police?"

"Oh, right, sorry." She rubbed her eyes. "I don't know, really. They just seem to be always complaining about how the police don't really care about anyone here in town—and then they were saying something about car thefts on another lot... But I'm not sure which one."

"Did they own multiple lots?"

"No, but they know the owners of all the car lots around here. It was a while back," she added. "I probably shouldn't have even mentioned it. I just thought that's why you were here. I figured they'd hire someone to help with the case since it was so..." Her voice trailed off, and her eyes glistened with moisture. "Brutal."

Heather and I exchanged glances. It was clear that Dahlia was troubled by what she had seen—her face was pale, colorless—and I don't like to further traumatize witnesses more than I have to.

"We're not here to rehash everything you've been through," Heather began, taking out Rossi's photo. "We have a pretty good feel for what happened, but we are interested in the man you saw. Was he alone, or was there someone with him?"

"I don't think there was anyone else with him," she said quickly. "I looked out and saw him run to one of the cars, then I shut the door. I didn't see anyone else in the car."

"And that's it?" I asked. "That's all you saw?"

She nodded, then said, "Yes, I closed the door and went to the office and... Well, Mr. Mallen... And... I..."

"It's okay," Heather said softly. "Take a deep breath."

Dahlia nodded and took a long, ragged breath. "He was by himself," she muttered.

"I'd like you to look at this photograph," Heather said, leaning forward and handing it to her. "Please look at it carefully. Could he be the man you saw?"

Dahlia frowned and stared at the photograph, slowly shaking her head. "No. Definitely not," she said, staring hard at the image.

"Have you ever seen this man before?" I asked.

She shook her head. "No, I don't think so. I mean... I might have, but he is kind of, you know, like... generic. I don't mean that in a bad way," she added quickly, visibly cringing at her own words. "I'm sorry. I don't know him." She handed the photo back to Heather.

"That's okay, Dahlia," Heather said, taking it from her.

"The man I saw had blond hair and blue eyes—and the nose and jaw are all wrong. He didn't look anything like that man in your picture."

"So, if you dyed this man's hair and put in blue contacts...?" Heather said.

Dahlia shook her head. "No. It wouldn't make any difference. The face is just all wrong. The complexion is off, too. The guy I saw was kinda pale, like a light complexion, and he had freckles."

"You got a good look at him, didn't you?" I said. "Have they set you up with a sketch artist?"

"No," she said. "I hung around in case they needed anything, but then they sent me home. They told me they'd gotten everything they needed from me. I guess I was probably an annoyance." Her cheeks flushed, and she looked down at her blue painted toenails. "Poor Mr. Mallen. I just wanted to help."

"And you have," Heather said. "We needed to know if it was the same man we're looking for, and now we know for sure that it's not. Thank you, Dahlia."

"If we were to connect you with a sketch artist, would you be willing to work with them?" I asked, figuring maybe I could talk the chief into it.

"Sure," Dahlia replied with a little head nod. "I'm fine with that. I want to help in whatever way that I can, and right now, I don't feel like I've been much help at all. Mr. Mallen was a good man for the most part."

"The most part?" I said, frowning. "What d'you mean?"

"Oh, um," she began, looking a little embarrassed. "He was really well-known in the town for being a good person, but he didn't pay the people outside of his circle all that great. I've worked there for five years as the office manager, and I still only make fifteen dollars an hour. He gave me a dollar raise two years ago, and I haven't had one since—but that's just me being petty, I guess." Dahlia gave us a sheepish look. "I shouldn't be complaining. Maybe if I didn't have so much student debt, it wouldn't be such a big deal."

"It's fine," Heather replied. "We understand... Was there anything else about Mr. Mallen that you want us to know before we go?"

Dahlia pursed her lips, looked thoughtful, and then slowly shook her head. "I don't... I don't think so. We haven't had a car theft before, but it's been talked about as a possibility... The dealership is right off the highway—but that was only when the security cameras went out. They've been finicky for the last couple of years. His father had the system installed more than twenty years ago... Mr. Mallen kept putting off the repair. He was kinda cheap."

"That's helpful information," Heather said. "Thank you for chatting with us. If you think of anything else, please contact us." She handed Dahlia her card.

Dahlia looked at it, then at Heather and nodded. "I'll show you out," she said.

She walked us to the door, opened it, stood to one side, and said, "Thank you for coming. It was so nice to meet you both."

I smiled at her, offered her my hand, and said, "It was nice to meet you too, Dahlia. Thank you for taking the time, and for your help."

"You're welcome," she said and closed the door.

We went down the steps and walked back to the car. I was...

DUPLICITY

I was wondering what the hell I was doing out there in the middle of nowhere, looking for a man who might or might not be dead, and I didn't know what next step to take.

We were far from home, far from New York, and didn't have a single solid lead. It was getting late. I was tired and... frustrated.

No more missing persons cases for me! I thought savagely.

23

HEATHER AND I DIDN'T SPEAK MUCH AS WE HEADED BACK toward the interstate, where I'd noticed a small café not far from where Dahlia Winters lived. I was bushed, and Heather wasn't looking so spry and cheerful, either. Was it because we were both just exhausted from the events of the last couple of days, or were we both stewing over the interview with Dahlia? Other than the fact that the killer wasn't Matteo Rossi, we'd not learned a damn thing other than Greg Mallen was a cheapskate.

"We need to call Doyle," Heather said as I pulled into a parking spot. "He might know who our guy is."

I grimaced at the thought of reading the mobster into the loop. "I not sure about that," I said. "He's a loose cannon, and I don't want him going off half-cocked. If he figures out who the killer is, there's no telling what he might do."

Heather turned to me as she unhooked her seat belt. "You really think he'd do that?"

"He held George at gunpoint, didn't he?" I said. "The man's a psychopath. Of course, he'd do that. Who the hell knows what he might do?"

She blew out a sharp breath. "You're probably right," she

said. "But I don't think you're thinking straight, Harry. If he knows who this guy is—and I'm pretty sure he does—we need to know. If he's mafia—Irish or Italian—we need to know. If he's on the same mission as we are, we need to know."

Inwardly, I shook my head. She was right; of course she was. But the thought of dealing directly with Doyle made my gut boil.

"I'll call Jacque and talk it over with her. Why don't you call Isabella Rossi and ask her if she knows of anywhere Matteo might have run off to? In the rush to get to the plane, I forgot to ask her. I was also assuming that Rossi was dead, and we still don't know that he isn't."

Heather nodded, sucking her bottom lip. "That's true," she said, "especially now that we know he doesn't have his driver's license. That alone makes me think he's probably dead."

"Maybe," I said, "but my gut is telling me otherwise. "I know it doesn't make sense, but it's what I've got, and right now, it's all I have to go on. And, you know something else that doesn't make sense? Doyle! What the hell is his game? The man shells out a hundred and fifty grand to find Rossi. Because he's his best friend? I'm not buying it. There's something rotten in the state of Denmark, and I want to know what it is."

Heather chuckled and took out her phone.

Me? I'd worked myself up thinking about Doyle. I stepped out of the car, took a deep breath, shrugged it off, and called Jacque. If it had been up to me, I'd have forgone something to eat. I was tired and antsy, and my head was aching.

"Hey, Harry," Jacque said. "How's it going?"

"It could be better," I said. "How about you?"

"With *your* case? Not so much. Tim is working on the footage the Charleston PD sent to us. The guy is not Rossi."

"That's what I'm thinking," I replied. "We talked to the

witness. She confirmed it. So who the hell is it, and why did he have Rossi's driver's license?"

I took a deep breath and rubbed my eyes with my free hand. I shook my head and looked up. The sun was hanging low in the sky, and it was beginning to cool off, though I felt more than a little clammy. I needed a shower and a change of clothes in the worst way.

Jacque chuckled. "I think you need to find a hotel and get some sleep. You sound tuckered out. As far as the license is concerned, until we either find Rossi, or his body, or the guy who killed Greg Mallen, there's no answer to it. You think Rossi's dead?"

I shook my head even though she couldn't see it. "Heather does. I don't."

Jacque was silent for a moment, then said, "Just because we haven't found a body doesn't mean he's still alive."

"Yeah, I know," I said. "It would be nice if we could get a sketch done of the perp. Our witness got a good look at him. How about you give Chief Wilbur a call and tell him Dahlia Winters got a good look at the guy and maybe he could get their sketch artist on it. He seemed reasonable enough."

"I'll do it," she said, "and I'll see if I can find someone local for you. If not, we have the budget. Maybe we can fly someone in from here."

"Hmm. It's a possibility, I suppose," I said skeptically. "I think we need to talk to Doyle, but I don't want to. I don't like the man."

"I hear you, Harry, but he might have answers." Jacque sounded as reluctant as I felt, but she had a point. "You want me to give him a call and see what he has to say?"

I thought it over for a few seconds. "Sure. Why not?" I hated to have my staff do something I should do myself, but, being as spent as I was, I'd make a mess of talking with Doyle.

"Come on, Harry. Lighten up. Sometimes you have to make lemonade out of the lemons." She chuckled. "I'll give him a call and see what he has to say. I'll keep you updated. That it, then?"

"Yes, I think so," I replied. "Talk to you later." And with that, I hung up and sent a text to Amanda, letting her know how the day had gone. I turned back to the car, but seeing that Heather was still on the phone, I waited until she'd finished.

Two minutes later, Heather hung up, stepped out of the car and joined me. She looked... exhausted.

"Well?" I asked her as we headed into the diner. "What did Isabella have to say for herself?"

Heather heaved a sigh and said, "Not much. Nothing at all that was helpful. She said she didn't know of anywhere he might have gone. He never went on vacation, and he rarely left Brooklyn, much less New York City."

"Terrific," I grumbled as I pulled the glass door open. "Well, maybe Jacque will have better luck. She's going to call Doyle."

Heather smiled. "I doubt he'll like that."

I shrugged, eyeing the *seat yourself* sign just inside the front entrance to the diner. "I hear ya," I said as I led Heather to a corner booth facing the entrance. I grabbed one of the menus from the clip and scanned the contents, shaking my head. Nothing sounded good.

What is wrong with me? I wondered, not for the first time that day. I never turned down a good hole-in-the-wall burger, and yet, here I was, tempted to order off the kids' menu to keep the portions small. In the end, I wound up ordering a grilled chicken sandwich, tater tots and a glass of water. Heather ordered a crispy chicken sandwich with onion rings and a Diet Coke.

I watched as she started in on her food with no little enthusiasm. Me? I eyed mine like it was a snake making ready to strike.

"You okay, Harry?" Heather asked, an onion ring just inches from her mouth. "You look like you're not feeling well."

"I'm fine," I said and picked up a tater tot and popped it into my mouth as if it was no big deal. "Just the miles catching up to me, I guess."

She nodded and bit a chunk out of the onion ring and chewed it slowly, watching me as I forced myself to swallow the greasy potato bite, ignoring how it made me feel worse rather than better. I did manage to finish most of the sandwich, though.

We finished our meal in relative silence, and I wondered if we needed to find a hotel in Charleston or if we'd be jetting off to somewhere new tonight. Part of me wanted to find a place to crash and get a good night's sleep; the other part was still hoping we'd get some answers. Though from where, I had no idea.

We finished up. I paid the bill, and we headed back to the car. The sun was setting in a blaze of color. The air was heavy; the quiet, palpable. *A portent of things to come?* I wondered as I opened the car door and climbed in.

"I wonder if Jacque has talked to Doyle yet," I said as I started the motor.

Heather chuckled. "For all we know, he might've followed us here."

"Not likely," I said, grinning at her. "Even he'd have trouble tailing a Gulfstream."

"Yeah, well, I wouldn't put anything past the guy," Heather said as she put on her seat belt. "And I have no idea where we're supposed to go from here, either."

I smiled and was about to make a smart remark when my phone rang. I took it from my pocket, glanced at the screen, and saw it was Jacque. "It's Jacque," I said, tapping the screen to accept the call. "Now maybe we'll get some answers."

24

"Doyle wants to talk to you, Harry," Jacque said brusquely. "And don't even argue with me because it's that or nothing."

I rolled my eyes. "He's on the other line, isn't he?"

"Bingo," Jacque huffed. "He's waiting for you to take the call."

I sighed. "Patch him through, Jacque. I'll put my phone on speaker so Heather can hear."

"Okay, please hold." She sounded like a receptionist, and I couldn't help but smile. Jacque would have slapped me silly for even thinking such a thing.

"So, the two of you are no longer in the Big Apple, then?" Doyle said. "I was wondering where dat big ole jet had taken off to. Your partner said you're in West Virginia. Now why would that be, I wonder?"

"There's been a murder at a car dealership here in Charleston," I said, looking at Heather.

"What? What the hell would that have to do with anyt'ng?" He sounded confused. "Matteo's not into morderin' people. You flying around on me money for no good reason, Starke? What d'you t'ink you're up to?"

"His driver's license was found on the floor next to the body," I snapped. "What does that tell you, Doyle?"

"Holy mother of God," Doyle responded. "How can that be? You t'ink it was him that done it?"

"No, I don't," I replied. "I think the license was planted to make it look that way. Either that or it was planted to throw us off. D'you know why he would have come to Charleston?"

"I do not," he replied. "I've never been to Charleston in me life, and I'm pretty sure Matteo hasn't either."

"I need answers, Doyle, and I need them now. This has gone on long enough. Someone knows something they're not telling, and my guess would be that it's you. So come on; give."

"Look... Harry," he said, "you've gotten me all wrong, so you have. I want to find him, and I have no idea why he would be in West Virginia any more than you do, or anyone else, for that matter." He sounded genuinely puzzled.

"There's somethin' bad goin' on here," he continued. I don't know what it is, but I do know one t'ing, Rossi would never have mordered anyone. He was nothin' but a mule; didn't want it any other way. We tried to toughen him up, so we did, but he would have none of it. So I know he wouldn't go off and murder someone. He's basically a good kid. I don't know what else to tell ya."

"Well, we're going to head back to Chattanooga," I said, making the decision on the fly. Heather looked at me, the corners of her mouth turned down in an expression of surprise, and I was sure Jacque was wondering what I was thinking, too.

"That's good to hear, Harry," Doyle replied. "Because I'm already back here in Chattanooga meself. I figured that's where you'd gone anyway."

I shut my eyes for a moment, ignoring the wave of nausea

that washed over me at hearing the Irish mob boss would be waiting for me when I got home.

"Are you, now?" I said dryly. "Then I guess I'll see you soon."

"That you will, Harry, me old son. That you will." And he hung up.

"You still there, Jacque?" I said.

"I am," she replied. "I guess I'll be seeing you soon, too."

"I guess you will…" I trailed off, then said, "I don't like the way he's watching our every move. Did I tell you he held George at gunpoint?"

"Oh, my God," she said. "Are you serious? Why? How…?"

"He forced George to let him into the car while he was waiting to pick us up. He just wanted an update, so he said. Though I think it was a powerplay, to remind us who was in charge."

"The man's psychotic," Jacque said. "He's dangerous."

"He is," I said, "but we already knew that. Look, I need to give the pilot a call. I'll see you tomorrow."

"Stay safe, Harry," she said. "You too, Heather."

We wrapped up the conversation, and two hours later, we were in the air headed back to Chattanooga. And I had never been more relieved to be on my way home.

Maybe it was because I knew Doyle was back in the city and I feared for my wife and daughter. Or maybe it was just that my stomach was still bothering me.

I leaned back in my seat as the jet took off into the night sky, and I began to sweat. I got up, went to the bathroom and washed my face, hoping I wasn't coming down with the flu.

"Harry," Heather said as I returned to my seat, "you look as pale as a ghost. Are you sure you're okay?"

I shook my head. "I'm not sure, Heather. I feel… queasy. Maybe it's all the crappy fast food we've eaten."

Heather nodded. "Maybe, but we eat it all the time when we're working on a case. It's never bothered you before."

I grimaced. "That's true," I said. "I hope I'm not coming down with something. Or maybe I'm just getting old." I chuckled and shut my eyes.

Heather chuckled. "Nah!" she said. "I figure you'll still be chasing bad guys when you're eighty."

"I'm hoping I'll be retired and living on an island in the Caribbean by then," I joked, though the thought sounded pretty good. Maybe there, I wouldn't have to deal with Irish mobsters like Finn Doyle tracking my every move. There was something about the guy I just didn't like.

Probably his mother, I thought. *Morrigan Doyle was as cunning and as slick as they come. She ran one hell of a Ponzi scheme, and while her son wasn't involved, I'm sure he learned a lot from her.*

A thought occurred to me. "Who's Finn Doyle's father?" I asked, turning to look at Heather and opening my eyes. "Doyle is Morrigan's maiden name."

Heather frowned as she looked at me. "I don't know. I guess I've never really thought about it. I thought Finn was... I don't know."

"I think we should find out," I said. "I'm curious. And it never hurts to know all the details about a client, especially this one."

She nodded. "Maybe his dad was never in the picture."

"Maybe not," I said. "But I don't feel like throwing theories around. We need facts. This case is all theories and conjecture, and I've had enough of working by guesswork. It's... It's frickin' exhausting."

I shut my eyes. Heather didn't reply. I figured maybe I'd been a bit harsh, but what I'd said *was* the truth. And, to beat all, my gut was churning like a barrel of stale beer. Was I really coming down with something nasty, or was it simply trying to tell me I was headed for something dark and stormy? *Oh, hell, maybe it's just trying to tell me to slow down and take a breather.*

I listened to the drone of the engines, hoping it would put me to sleep. It didn't. My mind, like my gut, was a maelstrom— thoughts moving through it so fast it was almost making me dizzy.

A case like Doyle's wasn't going to get solved overnight, though I was pretty sure Doyle was of the opinion that it should.

"You know, I think Catherine, Rossi's girlfriend, knows more than she's telling." Heather's voice pulled me out of the midden of groggy thoughts. "I've been checking out her social media," she continued, "and she's never posted anything about her missing boyfriend."

"He's paranoid about that kind of stuff," I said. "That's probably why. Maybe he figured she'd be in trouble if she plastered his face all over the internet."

Geez, here we go again, I thought. *More theories.*

"Or maybe she's doing her best to make sure he can't be found," Heather said thoughtfully. "Thinking back on our conversations with her, she never really appeared concerned for his safety, did she?"

"Forget it, Heather," I said. "I'm not going back to New York... But you do have a point. Maybe you should give her a call when we're back in the office tomorrow."

"She never bothered to report it to the police," Heather said. "I find that strange. Don't you?"

"Not really," I said. "Not when you consider there are two factions of the mafia involved. Maybe one, or both, don't want him found."

Heather nodded. I smiled. I could almost see the wheels turning inside her head. She was trying to put the pieces together, even though I'd told her to quit with the theories, at least until we knew more. But I could tell something about the case was resonating with her, and as much as I wanted to ask about it, my body was telling me to shut the hell up and get some rest.

And so I sat there with my eyes shut tight, counting down the minutes to when we'd be back on solid ground and I'd be home with my family. I knew something was wrong with me. I ran my sweaty hands along the tops of my jeans, willing away the growing nausea. I could only imagine what Heather was thinking as she watched me from across the aisle. I *knew* I was looking pretty damn sick, and I was.

I managed to hold it together until the plane touched down in Chattanooga, and I couldn't have been more relieved to set foot again on solid ground.

Heather offered to drive me home. I almost refused, but I quickly gave in as my stomach began to cramp.

It turned out that even Harry Starke could catch the stomach flu.

25

THE NEXT TWO DAYS PASSED BY IN A BLUR. WHILE I WAS SICK, I was out of touch with my team, and I'm sure Jacque and Amanda had much to do with that. I spent the first forty-eight hours bedridden, and after that, I was weak as a kitten, but at least I was able to move around.

"You look much better this morning," Amanda said as I stepped into the kitchen on the third morning, feeling slightly nauseous but also hungry. "I had a few moments there I thought you might need a hospital," she added, smiling.

"Imagine that," I muttered as I pulled out a chair.

"Well, I didn't think you were going to die. But you sure did act like you were," she said with a laugh, giving me a funny look. "I'd offer you some coffee, but..."

"No coffee," I said. "Just a glass of water."

"Coming right up." She grabbed a glass, filled it up with filtered water from the fridge, and then set it down in front of me. "It's a good thing it's a weekend, or, knowing you, you'd be headed into work."

"I probably should be," I said, then took a sip of water.

Amanda watched with a look of concern on her face.

"How're you feeling?"

"Fine. You don't have to watch over me like Jade." I winked at her and then took another swallow of water.

Amanda sighed. "Well, Maria has Jade today. I know it's a weekend, but I wasn't sure how you'd be feeling, and Maria had tickets to the Disney on Ice program."

"Ah, Jade will love that," I said, glancing up at the clock. It was after ten. I'd damn near slept the day away, but I tried not to let it bother me.

"So, you know that Rossi fellow you're looking for?" Amanda began as though she'd been reading my mind. "His face is all over the news with that West Virginia murder."

I rubbed my forehead, not surprised or happy about it. "He'll more than likely go into hiding then," I said, "and they're going to be swamped with bogus tips. You know how this works. They'll be looking all over West Virginia for him, and my guess is he's long gone."

"You're not very positive about this, are you?" Amanda laughed, shaking her head at me. "I was hoping that it would work out in your favor and maybe alleviate some of the pressure. With his face plastered all over the media, it's almost a guarantee they'll catch him... if he's still alive."

I considered what she'd said for a moment, and while I would've been more than happy if the media was able to lead the authorities to Rossi, I figured it wasn't likely to happen. In which case, I was pretty damn sure Doyle wasn't going to let up.

Inwardly, as I stared into my half empty glass, I wondered what else we could do. There was no telling where Rossi might be. He could have been in any one of a dozen states from West Virginia to Florida. We were in limbo until something broke, and at that point I couldn't see that happening.

"Please don't worry about it today," Amanda said, breaking

into my thoughts and patting my arm. "You'll be back in the office Monday, and then you can figure it out. For now, you need to rest."

"I've been resting for the last two days," I reasoned with her, chuckling.

She shot me a dirty look. "Uh-huh, and you were so sick, all you did was sleep and complain—"

"I get it, I get it," I said, interrupting her. "How have you been?"

She shrugged. "I took the time off. There's not a lot going on at work right now. Well, other than the usual local excitement: consternation over the number of potholes in the county roads, and the like."

"No potential serial killers popping up, then?"

"Thankfully, no." She put her elbow on the table and leaned her chin in the palm of her hand as she stared at me. "That was a nasty bout of the flu," she said. "I'm glad you're feeling better."

I frowned and said, "I hope I didn't give it to you."

"Well, if Jade didn't pass it to me, then I'm probably immune."

She gave me a playful look. I shook my head and said to her, "I don't think anyone is immune to a stomach bug."

"Maybe not. Maybe I just wash my hands more often than you."

I was about to make a smart reply to that when she changed the subject and said, "I think Rossi has upset someone and has dropped off the grid. I think—"

"You think he's still alive?" I finished for her. I shrugged. "Maybe. Maybe not. No one's heard a peep from him, unless I missed something over the past couple of days. All the indicators point to him being dead... But what bothers me the most is why the hell is Doyle so intent on finding him? Friends don't fork over a hundred and fifty grand to find a friend. It makes no sense."

"True." Amanda leaned against the counter. "And you're wrong when you said I think he's alive; I don't. The driver's license thing makes me think he's *not*. That has to be a plant. Surely, he's not so stupid as to drop it after shooting someone dead. I mean, he would have had to have taken his wallet out of his pocket, the license out of the wallet, and then dropped it where everyone could see it. He might just as well have called it in himself and then confessed. It just doesn't gel... does it?"

"Or," I said, "he could have been killed and his wallet lifted from the body. It happens all the time, but the question then becomes, why?" I paused for a second, thinking, then sighed, looked up at her and said, "I think it could go either way, but my gut's telling me he's still out there somewhere, running for his life."

"I did some digging into the family's Facebook pages," Amanda said hesitantly. "I don't think Catherine, his girlfriend, is a fan."

That surprised me. "Really? I had no idea you were looking into it."

"Well, you piqued my curiosity, and you know me." She blushed, shrugging her shoulders. "It's what I do for a living, as you well know. D'you want me to show you?"

I smiled at my wife. "You know I do."

She stood up, hurried away, and returned two minutes later with her laptop. She set it down on the table in front of me and leaned over me.

"Let me see..." she said as she pulled up Catherine's Facebook page. "I went through her photos, all of them, and there are a lot, but there are none of Rossi and very few of the baby... Have you seen the child, by the way?"

"No," I replied. "Facebook was the first place Tim looked.

We all thought she didn't have pictures of Rossi posted because she was respecting his wishes to keep a low profile... What do you mean about the kid?"

She gave me a serious look. "Have you looked at a photograph of her son?"

"No..."

"Here. Take a look." She navigated to a picture I hadn't seen before and said, "This is her son."

It was a picture of a toddler with a cute smile. I turned my head to look up at her and said, "This is Rossi's son?"

"Yep," she replied. "That's Matteo Rossi's son."

I frowned and looked again at the green eyes and blond hair. "This can't be right... Or maybe it is. I don't know. Genetics?"

"Or *maybe* he's not his son."

"That's..." I stared at the photo, searching for any resemblance. "Let me grab my picture of Rossi." I stood up, feeling a fresh surge of energy, and went to my office, grabbed the photo and returned to the kitchen.

I compared it to the image of the kid who was supposed to be Matteo Rossi's. I shook my head and set it down in the corner of the screen.

And we stood and looked at the two images in silence.

"I need to get back to work," I muttered.

26

AMANDA CONVINCED ME THERE WAS NO NEED TO GO RUSHING out to the office, that I should take Sunday off and rest up for another twenty-four hours and, reluctantly, I agreed. I did, however, send a message to Tim along with a photo of Matteo's son. And I couldn't help but wonder how he missed it. True, Amanda's a successful investigative journalist, but Tim's... Ah, never mind. It didn't matter, and once Monday morning rolled around, I was up at my usual time at a little after six, though still feeling a decided lack of energy.

That being so, I opted for a swim in the pool instead of my usual morning run. It was a clear morning and the view of the city below as the sun peeked above the horizon was spectacular. I did my twenty laps and climbed out of the pool feeling better than I had in more than a week. My thought was that I succumbed to the bug because I was worn out and my resistance was low.

I took a quick shower, then joined Amanda, Jade, and Maria in the dining room for eggs, bacon, and biscuits.

Barely had I begun to eat when my phone started buzzing.

Probably someone wondering why I'm not at the office yet, I thought as I picked it up and looked at the screen.

"Huh! It's Kate," I said and answered it.

"Kate," I said. "What's up?"

"Harry. You feeling better? I heard through the grapevine that you caught the dreaded stomach bug."

"Better than I deserve," I quipped. "What's up, Kate? I know you're not calling me just to check on my health." I stood up and excused myself from the table, going outside through the kitchen, breathing in the crisp mountain air. It was already eight-thirty, and I was late.

"Well," she said, drawing out the word, "you're right. I think I might have some information for you."

I leaned up against the doorjamb. "Do tell," I said.

"Traffic happened upon a stolen car, a white Chevy Blazer, early this morning. Someone called it in. Said it was causing a problem. Anyway, short story even shorter, the officers ran the plate and it came back as registered to one Jose Alamos of Parkersburg, West Virginia. Trouble is, Alamos died three years ago in a road accident. The license plate belonged to him. So, they ran the VIN number, and it came back as registered to the Mallen Dealership in Charleston, West Virginia."

"A white Chevy Blazer, you said?" I asked.

"Yep. I figured you might find that interesting since there's a BOLO out for your missing man, Rossi. But I have more. You ready?"

"Okay. Hit me."

"It was parked across the street from the home of… Carmen Rossi."

I nearly dropped the phone. "No shit?" I said, stunned. "Is she related to Matteo Rossi?"

"Yeah, but it's distant. Maybe an aunt once or twice removed. She's lived here a long time, and at the same address.

I'm heading over there to chat with her. You want to join me? The tow truck's about forty minutes out. If you're quick, you can take a look at the car, too."

"You know I do. Send me the address, and I'll be there as soon as I can. Don't let them tow that car until I get there."

"Got it. See you soon, then… Oh, and make sure you keep your distance. I don't have time to catch any bugs. I have a vacation coming up."

"Geez, are you serious?" I joked and hung up the phone. I didn't give myself a lot of time to process what I'd just learned, but I knew that I'd have to relay the information to Jacque as I drove. I needed a background check on Carmen Rossi. ASAP.

I went quickly back into the house, grabbed my weapon, slipped it into its holster under my arm, slipped into my jacket and grabbed my laptop bag.

"Off in a rush?" Amanda asked as I headed for the garage.

"Yeah," I replied. "That was Kate. It seems we might have a lead."

"Oh?" She raised her eyebrows and folded her arms.

I nodded. "Right here in Chattanooga, would you believe?" I told her and gave her a peck on the lips. Then I kissed the top of Jade's head, told Maria goodbye, wished everyone a good Monday and told them I'd see them that evening.

I hit the garage door opener and headed straight for my car. I wasn't sure what I thought about the Chevy turning up in Chattanooga. It was yet another in a long list of enigmas. One thing I did know was that I wasn't heading back to New York anytime soon. The mere thought of flying made my stomach swirl.

I climbed into the car and started the engine, turning the radio down. I was in no mood to listen to music. I waited for the phone to connect to the Bluetooth system and then backed out, telling the system to call Jacque.

"I was wondering if we needed to call for a welfare check,"

Jacque answered, laughing. "But seriously, Harry, are you feeling any better today? We've tried our best to leave you alone."

"Yeah. I know you have, and I appreciate it," I said as I turned left on Scenic Highway and headed down the mountain, following the GPS coordinates to an address in a neighborhood on the north side of the river. "I'm okay. But listen, I just had a call from Kate. They found the Chevy, here in Chattanooga. I'm heading that way now to meet Kate and get a look at it. It's parked outside a Carmen Rossi's house."

I could tell by the silence I'd hit a nerve, and then she said, "Sorry, who?"

"Carmen Rossi," I repeated, smiling. "Did you know Matteo Rossi has an aunt who lives here in the city?"

"You're kidding…" I could hear the surprise in her voice. "No. Of course not. I never… I had no idea he had connections to Chattanooga. How did we miss this?"

"I don't know, but my guess is there are a great many Rossis out there. It's quite a common Italian name."

I thought about that, tapping the steering wheel as I drove across the Market Street bridge into North Chattanooga. "It would be an aunt on his father's side… Hmm, maybe we should dig deeper into his father."

"Maybe," Jacque agreed, then said, "D'you think he was there, after all? At the dealership in Charleston?"

"Well, we know the car was," I replied, "and the blond guy, if that's what you're asking." I chuckled. "But Rossi? He could have been outside, I suppose. And maybe he'd teamed up with Blondie. Or maybe Blondie's looking for him, too and paying aunty a visit."

"That doesn't strike me as highly likely," she said. "What're the odds that Rossi *wasn't* at the crime, and then the stolen car shows up at his aunt's house? I think he was there."

"Well, it's something," I said. "We'll know more soon, I'm sure."

"Should I call the dealership and let them know the car's been found?" she asked.

"Nah," I said as I turned into the subdivision. "Better let the Charleston PD take care of it. I'm sure Kate's people have let them know they found it. We need to focus on finding whoever it was that parked it here."

"You do realize they could still be in the house," Jacque said. "If they're not, they must have left in another vehicle."

"I'm sure Carmen Rossi will be able to provide the answer to that," I said as I pulled up behind Kate's car. Samson, her dog, had his head hanging out the window, his tongue lolling out.

I put the car in park and stepped out to be greeted by a blast of hot summer air. I had never been a fan of the heat, but at least it was a clear day with no rain in the forecast.

I wanted to get a look at the car before they towed it. There was an outside chance we might find something helpful, though I wasn't holding my breath. And there was yet another outside chance, as Jacque said, that the blond-haired man we'd been searching for would be waiting for us inside Carmen Rossi's home.

Though, something in my gut was telling me it wasn't going to be that easy. But then, when was it ever?

27

"Good morning, Samson," I greeted the big German Shepherd, patting his head as Kate stepped out of her unmarked cruiser.

He snapped his chops and gifted me with his signature toothy grin.

"Kate," I said and gave her a nod.

"Harry," she said. "For someone who was reportedly at death's door two days ago, you're looking remarkably chipper."

"Death's door?" I asked, frowning. "Who told you that?"

"I was joking, Harry, just joking. You do look well, though."

"Thanks," I said dryly. "You don't look bad yourself."

And she really didn't. She was wearing jeans and a white blouse with her gun and badge clipped to her belt. It kinda reminded me of times gone by, but that's another story; a lot of stories, in fact.

"Thanks," she said, just as dryly. "So, let's take a look at the car before we start door-knocking." She brushed aside a lock of blond hair that had fallen over her eye.

"So what's got you working an abandoned vehicle, Captain?" I teased as we approached the white Chevy. "I would have thought something like this would be way below your pay grade."

She shot me a glare. "You know damn well what it's about," she snapped. "It's connected to a murder, and the chief has been talking to his counterpart in Charleston. Turns out he knows the guy. So it's eyes on, T's crossed, I's dotted."

"Charming," I muttered, not missing being one of the boys in blue one little bit, or the politicking that went along with it.

Sure, I had to play by the rules, just as they did, but I was free of all the BS, and I made my own decisions without some idiot with more rank peering over my shoulder.

"I was surprised to learn you were working a missing person's case on Rossi, though," Kate said, handing me a pair of latex gloves. The tow truck driver was standing by, chatting with the two uniformed officers.

"Yeah, well, it's not something I feel like bragging about," I said as I opened the front passenger-side door.

"I did a little checking into this Matteo Rossi," she said. "As far as I can tell, he's clean. No rap sheet. Nothing. And no one's reported him missing, not officially anyway."

"Not just clean," I said. "He's a blank sheet. I was hired to find him by a friend of his, one Finn Doyle. Name sound familiar?"

Her head snapped round to look at me. "Not—"

"Yup," I said. "That's the one. He's Morrigan Doyle's son, and he's one of the top dogs in the Irish mob. And don't even ask. It's a long story and not one I want to talk about right now."

"Oh boy," Kate said, shaking her head. "You do get yourself into some messes, don't you, Harry?"

I didn't bother to answer, mostly because she was right. I'd been kicking myself ever since I didn't throw Doyle out of my office on his ass that day he'd walked in, grinning as if he had all the answers.

"Rossi's an Italian name—"

"And he has ties to the Italians, too," I said, cutting her off. "The name Enzo Massino mean anything to you?"

"No… I don't think so," she said. "Oh wait… yes!"

"He runs one of the smaller New York families," I said. "Rossi's mother is tight with him. It's one convoluted mess of a case."

I was going to say more, but it was at that point I noticed a piece of paper under the driver's seat. I reached in and picked it up. It was a cash receipt for gas from a station here in town.

"What ya got?" Kate asked.

"Just a gas receipt," I said and handed it to her.

Other than that, the inside of the car was pristine. I stepped back and closed the door. If there had been two people traveling in it, there was no way to tell. Maybe forensics could, but I couldn't.

"Hmm, just ten bucks' worth," Kate said. "That tells a story. He must have been out of gas… No key. Hah!" She looked at the receipt and said, "I know that one. It's just off the Interstate in Ooltewah. There should be camera footage."

She slipped the receipt into a baggy. "Maybe we'll get lucky. You never know."

"I really don't," I said as I walked around to the driver's side and opened the rear door. It, too, was clean. I checked the rear storage area. It was the same.

"Whoever it was went to great lengths to keep it clean," Kate commented as I closed the back hatch and shook my head. "It's like they wanted us to find it."

"Of course they did," I said. "They parked right smack dab in the middle of the neighborhood. I don't understand why they didn't leave it in a parking lot somewhere. It would've been much harder to find." I was thinking out loud, and the more I thought about it, the more my gut was telling me the location had been carefully chosen, and I didn't like that feeling.

"Excuse me," a voice called out from behind me. We both spun around to see a dark-headed woman I assumed to be in her mid-thirties walking toward us. It took only a glance for me to see she was related to Matteo Rossi.

Why does his son look nothing like him? I wondered.

I pushed the thought away and turned to meet her.

"Good morning," Kate said. "I'm Captain Gazzara, Chattanooga PD, and you are?"

She glanced warily at Kate, then at me, then nodded and said, "I'm Carmen Rossi-Santiago. I saw the police officers and was hoping someone could help me. Someone stole my car last night. I need to report it. I didn't realize it was gone until I saw what was happening out here." She gestured to the tow truck.

"Why don't we go inside where we can talk?" I suggested.

"Well, umm… Uh…" Her voice trailed off, but then she nodded. "Very well, but we have to keep it down. My daughter's asleep. She's only two months old."

"Thank you," Kate said, smiling at her. "We'll be quiet."

Carmen nodded, wrapping her cardigan tighter and folded her arms, then turned and we followed her to the front door of a modern, two-story home.

I thought about the small place that Isabella Rossi lived in. It was very different to this rather upscale home, and I had to wonder if they even knew each other.

"We can sit in the dining room if that's okay?" she said, holding the door open for us.

"Of course," Kate replied. And Carmen ushered us into a large dining room, brightly lit by windows on the right side and far end.

"Please, sit down," she said. And we did. We sat at the dark cherry dining table beneath a rather intimidating glass chandelier.

"Would you like something to drink, coffee, perhaps? Water?" she asked as she lingered at the threshold.

"No. Thank you," Kate replied.

"No thanks," I said, even though I could've used some coffee.

She came in and sat down opposite us, her hands clasped together on the table in front of her.

"So," she said, "my car—"

"Before we get to that, Mrs. Santiago," Kate said, cutting her off. She set her phone to record and placed it on the table in front of her. "I need to inform you I'm going to record the interview for the record. It's no big deal. It just keeps the record straight. Is that all right with you?"

She nodded hesitantly, then said, "I suppose so, but why—"

"Are you related to Matteo Rossi?" Kate asked, cutting her off again.

"Yes," she replied. "He's my nephew. My older brother is Matty's father, but—"

"When did you last see him?" Kate asked.

"I haven't," she replied. "Not since he was little. Why—"

"So you're not close to the rest of the family?" Kate said.

"The New York side of the family?" she said. "No. We haven't talked all that much since we moved out of the old family home in New York. My father moved us out of Brooklyn to Long Island. We saw each other on holidays. I left New York when I met my husband at Columbia University. Then we moved here. This is where he's from… That was more than ten years ago. Other than Facebook, I don't keep up with them."

"And you haven't heard from Matteo in the last few days?" Kate pressed.

"No. I told you I hadn't," she said and leaned back in her

chair. "What's this about, Captain? I thought this was about my car?"

"It is," Kate replied, "in a roundabout way. The car across the road was stolen in West Virginia. We think by Matteo Rossi. I think he dumped it here and took yours."

She opened her mouth to speak, then snapped it shut again, staring at Kate, her eyes wide.

"Do you happen to know if any of your neighbors have video doorbells?" Kate asked.

She was silent for a moment, then said, "I do, actually. Well, not a doorbell. A security camera. I didn't even think to look at it. But why would Matty—"

"We'll look at your security system in a moment," Kate said. "But in answer to your question, Matteo is a person of interest in a murder in West Virginia."

Carmen stared at Kate, and I watched as the color drained from her face.

"I... don't..." she stuttered, then bit her bottom lip, her eyes wide. Then she seemed to gather some strength. She sat up straight and said, "Matty? You can't be serious. There's no way. You must have made a mistake."

"You say you're not close," I said, "but you seem shocked that Matteo might be involved."

"Of course I'm shocked," she snapped. "Wouldn't you be? This is my family you're talking about. As far as I know, Matty has never been in any kind of trouble, much less murder. Now, if you said it was Micah. That might be different. Even then, I'd find it hard to believe. But Matty? Never! And why would he come here? They don't even know where I live. They've never been here."

"When was the last time you saw any of them?" I asked.

"At my brother's funeral a couple of years ago, and that was just his sister Isabella and one of her friends, Enzo somebody."

Kate nodded, her expression stoic. "And you heard nothing last night?" she said. "How about your husband? Is he at work?"

She nodded. "He wasn't here last night. He left yesterday afternoon for Chicago. He's on a business trip. He'll be home late this evening, thank God."

I looked at her. She looked away. There were dark circles around her eyes. She looked exhausted.

Maybe it's the new motherhood thing, I thought. *Or maybe she knows more than she's telling.*

"Why don't we take a look at that footage?" Kate suggested.

"Yes, of course," Carmen said and pushed back from the table. "It's on the computer in Aldo's office. If you'll follow me, please."

We followed her down the hallway to a small, tastefully decorated office where she leaned over the desk, tapped the mouse to wake up the computer, and then navigated to the security system.

"There," she said and stood back. "I'll let you guys figure it out. I don't really know how it works, but I know that the camera on the front of the house has a wide view of the street and our front yard."

Kate sat down, put her hand on the mouse and flipped through the views until she found the correct camera. Carmen was right. The camera was located high up on the corner of the house, offering a wide view of the street.

Kate rolled the footage back twelve hours. "Do you always park outside the garage?" Kate asked, nodding at the black Ford Explorer. "I'm assuming that's your car."

"Yeah, our garage is full of stuff," she said, her right hand supporting her left elbow, her left hand at her mouth. "I've been promising myself I'd clean it up, but somehow I've never gotten around to it. I didn't think it was a big deal… to park outside. Nothing ever happens here."

"What about your husband?" I asked. "I take it his car is at the airport."

She nodded and sucked her bottom lip. "He has two cars: his BMW and a car he's fixing up. It's in the garage, too."

Kate nodded and went back to the video. "We can check out the garage on the way out," she said.

She fast forwarded the footage until, at eleven minutes to three in the morning, headlights appeared from the southern end of the street. The car parked across the street, and the lights shut off. It was the Chevy Blazer.

After a moment or two, the driver's side door opened—the car was parked on the wrong side of the road—and someone wearing a hoodie with the hood up stepped out and tossed something into the grass.

The person—it was impossible to see who it was, or even if it was a man or a woman—then walked across the street and onto the Santiago driveway.

"What did he just do?" I asked.

"The Chevy keys," Kate said, not looking up. "We found them this morning. I thought it was odd at the time, but now it looks even more odd. Why would he do that?"

And it only got stranger as the person walked directly up the driveway to the Ford Explorer and glanced around, keeping his head down. Then he opened the door, climbed in, started the engine, backed out and drove away heading south. He was in and away in a matter of seconds.

"Oh, my God," Carmen gasped. Then she sobbed, shook her head and whispered, "I guess... I guess I must have left the key in it. Aldo is going to kill me."

She sounded genuine enough. In fact, she sounded desperately upset, but something about it didn't sit right with me, though I couldn't put my finger on what it was. "Can you send us a copy of the footage?" I asked.

"Sure, um, I think so. I don't really know how," Carmen replied, wiping her eyes. "But I'm sure I can figure it out."

"I have an SD card," Kate said, quickly taking it from her wallet and inserting it into the computer tower. "I'll make you a copy, Harry." As soon as she plugged it in, her phone began to ring. She hesitated for a second, then took it out and answered it.

"Gazzara."

She listened for a moment and then stood up and left the room, the phone at her ear.

I took it upon myself to sit down and copy the data as far back as the time of the murder in West Virginia. If there were comings and goings to and from the Santiago house, I wanted to know it.

By the time I had it copied, Kate had returned. "We need to wrap it up here," she said. "Now! Come on." Then she turned to Carmen and said, "We'll be in touch." She handed her a card and said, "Please call me if you need anything or think of anything else that might help."

I grabbed the SD card, stood up and followed Kate out of the house.

"What the hell, Kate? I hadn't—"

"They've just located an abandoned black Ford Explorer," she said as we ran to her car. "And a body."

28

A BODY?

That's all I managed to get out of her before she jumped into her unmarked cruiser and streaked away, lights flashing, siren screaming.

I followed Kate to a Conway Inn & Suites motel off I-24 on the west side of the city, wondering if we were going to find the mortal remains of Matteo Rossi or the man who killed Greg Mallen. Either way, there was one thing of which I was certain: If someone had killed the person we saw leave in the Ford Explorer, it meant that someone involved in all this was just a few steps ahead of us.

I called Jacque as I drove, but the call went straight to voicemail. I hung up and tried Heather.

"Hey, Harry," she answered on the second ring. "Jacque told me about the stolen car turning up. Were you able to figure anything out?"

"No," I replied. "But someone stole Carmen Rossi's car, and it looks like whoever it was has turned up dead. I'm following Kate to the crime scene. I just tried to call Jacque. Where is she?"

"She's back there with Tim. They're working on that photo."

"Gotta go, Heather," I said as I took the off-ramp and saw the cruisers and the CSI in the motel parking lot. "Tell Jacque I'll call her as soon as I know something. Oh, and hold off on the phone calls. I don't want to give anyone a heads-up."

I hung up and pulled up behind Kate's cruiser. The parking lot was a hive of activity.

I opened the door, stepped out, and joined Kate and Samson. They were already out of the cruiser waiting for me.

"Sorry," I said. "I had to make a phone call."

I looked around the parking lot. The Explorer was parked on the far west side, away from the rest of the cars. It stood out like a sore thumb. Even from across the lot, I could see the driver's side window was shattered, and I could see someone I assumed to be a man slumped over the steering wheel.

An officer approached us. "Good morning, Captain, Samson..." He paused, looked at me and then continued. "Lieutenant Willis is over there."

I left the two of them talking and went to where Mike Willis was standing beside the passenger side open door.

"Mike, it's been a while," I said, patting him on the shoulder as I took a pair of latex gloves from the box on the Explorer's hood.

"Harry," he said brightly, with a look of surprise on his face. "How the heck are you? Long time no see. What are you doing here? You have a connection to... this?"

"Yeah," I said. "You could say that. I left Kate over there. You found anything yet?"

He nodded, gesturing to an open wallet on the passenger seat. "Driver's license for Nick Waters of New York City. Doesn't look like he has any other form of identification on him, but he's definitely the guy in the license picture."

"May I?" I said.

He nodded, and I picked up the wallet, noting the photo. It was hard to tell if it was the man in the footage in West Virginia, but it could have been.

"Doc is on his way," Mike said.

"Are there cameras?" I asked.

He snorted a laugh and said, "At this place? Are you kidding?" He sighed, shook his head, and then said, "Sorry. Yes, there are, but they're not working. If they were, this place would be out of business. The type of clientele... Well, you know what I mean."

"I do," I said as I peered into the car. There was a car seat in the back, which further confirmed it was the Explorer stolen from the Santiagos in North Chattanooga. I looked around, searching for... anything. I leaned in and looked down between the seats and the console, and something black caught my eye. It was a cell phone. "Aha," I said as I struggled to get my fingers far enough down to grab it.

A couple of seconds later I stepped back, triumphantly waving it in the air.

"I would've found that," Mike muttered, "eventually."

"I know you would've." I chuckled, stepping away from the car, and swiping across the screen, hoping... And it was. It was unlocked. I opened the recent call log and saw there were a *lot* of calls to the same New York City number.

Why not? I thought, as I pulled out my own phone and tapped the number into a group text to the team, and asked if anyone could identify it. I expected it to take some time, given they'd probably have to do some searching. However, before I had time to put my phone back in my pocket, it buzzed. I had an answer from Heather.

Isabella Rossi.

Shocked, I went back to the victim's—so I assumed— phone. There were at least fifty calls back and forth between the two over the last week alone. However, the text messages—if there had been any—had all been deleted. *What the hell?*

I pondered the thought for a few moments longer as I stared at the body still slumped over the steering wheel. It was clear he'd been killed by a single shot to the head. I took in the blueish hue to his lips. I walked closer to the car, reached in and touched his wrist.

Hmm… no rigor mortis. I glanced around the parking lot.

I was no Doc Sheddon, but even I knew this man hadn't been dead long, and that meant that whoever was responsible for it might not be far away. I turned to one of the uniformed officers as I laid a gloved hand on the hood of the Explorer. "Was the engine warm when you got here?"

He looked at me and said, "The engine was running."

The engine was running? I frowned and looked again around the parking lot.

"And did anyone see anything?" I asked as I handed the phone to Mike and turned away. "Who made the call?"

"The hotel manager said he thought he heard shots sometime around ten, but he didn't see anything, and so far we haven't found anyone who did. It was called in by someone who said he was one of the guests, but he didn't give his name and he's nowhere to be found."

"Anyone check the front desk for a name?" I asked.

"Sure," the officer replied. "But this place being what it is…"

"I get it," I said. "So, what you're telling me is that someone walked up and shot this man in the head, in broad daylight, and *no one* saw it?" I shook my head. "That's impossible. Someone had to have seen *something.*"

"It's happened before," Kate said as she joined me. "Though not all that often. But if no one is looking… And if no one wants to get involved…"

"Yeah, I know, but still," I muttered, and I told her about the phone and its implications. I'd just finished when Doc Sheddon joined us and dumped his big black bag at my feet.

"Greetings, Kate," he said, smiling. "You, too, Harry. Funny finding you here."

"I don't know what's so funny about it," I shot back at him.

"Ha ha," he said and peeked into the open driver's side door. "Gunshot wound to the head, I see. How original!" He leaned in to take a closer look. "Not too long ago, either." He grabbed the dead man's wrist. "Less than a couple of hours, tops. That's just a preliminary guess, of course."

I looked at my watch. It was eleven forty-three.

"Good guess," I said. "The motel manager claims he heard the shot around ten this morning."

Doc nodded but said nothing.

I looked at Kate and said, "I'm thinking the killer hopped right back onto I-24 and took off."

"They've already searched around the parking lot and the motel," she said thoughtfully. "So far they haven't found a damn thing, which isn't totally surprising, not if the killer simply drove up, took the shot, and then drove away again."

"Maybe," I said, leveling with her. "Who is this guy? I mean, we know his name, and judging by all the phone calls, he knows Isabella Rossi—"

"Kate, Harry. I think I found something you're gonna be interested in," Mike Willis called. "In fact, I don't just think. I *know* you're going to want to see this."

I turned around and stepped to the passenger side of the car, where Mike was holding what appeared to be a crumpled manilla file folder.

"What is it?" I asked.

"The victim was sitting on it," Doc said, grinning, "which I find rather strange, but then, I've seen stranger."

"I'm sure you have," I said. And then, as Mike set the folder down on the hood of the Explorer, I saw the words written in black Sharpie across the top. Matteo Rossi.

"That leaves nothing to the imagination, does it?" I muttered. I slipped my index finger into the file and then flipped it open, struck by the sheer number of sheets of paper. On the top sheet were listed a half-dozen GPS coordinates, more than two dozen phone numbers, and *this* motel's address. "What the hell…"

"No kidding," Kate commented, leaning over me to get a closer look. "This guy must have been tracking him."

I flipped through the papers, noting that the file was just as complete as our own. "This file contains information about every member of Matteo Rossi's family, even Carmen Rossi. See? That's her address and phone number."

Kate and I exchanged looks. "I need to make a copy of this file," I said, and I took out my phone and began snapping pictures of every single document in the file. Then I sent them all to the group chat.

I also added Nick Waters' name and told Tim to drop everything until he'd found out who the guy was.

Our wild goose chase was getting wilder by the minute.

29

Where the hell was he between three in the morning when he picked up the Explorer and ten o'clock when someone shot him in the head?

The thought bounced around inside my head as I backed away from the scene, intending to call Heather. But then, something, or rather someone, caught my eye across the street. A man was standing outside the Italian restaurant, watching, and something about the *way* he was watching hit a nerve. And I had to go find out for myself.

Checking for traffic, I started across the road, not even thinking about the fact that he must know I was walking toward him. I couldn't make out the man's face beneath the black ball cap, but he made it clear he didn't want to chat. He saw me coming, spun around and took off running.

Oh crap! I thought as I ran after him.

Now running, as you know, is my number one pastime, but, having just gotten over a nasty bout of the stomach flu, I wasn't ready for a full-on chase. Nevertheless, I sucked in extra oxygen as I ran at an easy pace, letting my quarry wear himself out, so I hoped.

"Hey! I just want to talk," I shouted after him.

But he didn't slow down. He moved quickly through the restaurant parking lot, and as he put more and more distance between him and me, I began to realize I was in a race I wasn't going to win.

I could see the guy was young, even though he was wearing a hoodie. He was also athletic. *Young and fast, damn it.*

I sped up, pushed on, and began to gain on him. I chased him behind a veterinary clinic, and as he scaled a fence, he glanced back at me and I saw his face.

Matteo Rossi.

"Matteo. Stop!" I shouted as I scaled the fence. He took off like a scalded rabbit into the trees. I took a few more strides then gave it up; he was too fast for me in my post-flu condition.

"Damn it all to hell!" I shouted. I leaned against a tree, bent over, head down, hands on my knees, gasping for breath, and frustrated beyond measure.

It would've been hard to catch up with Rossi even on my best day; the man was fifteen years younger than me and in great shape. But then I consoled myself with the thought that though the chase was a failure, I now knew one thing for certain: Matteo Rossi was alive and well—and right here in Chattanooga, Tennessee.

But why? Why is he here? What are his connections to this city? Is he closer to Carmen than she would admit? Did he kill Nick Waters? And who the hell killed Greg Mallen? Waters? If so, why? And what the hell does Doyle have to do with it all? And Waters... Who and what the hell is he? And then it hit me—

It was at that moment, as I leaned back against the tree, still trying to recover, when I heard Kate call, "Harry. Where are you?"

"Over here," I croaked as Samson came bounding through the

trees. I slid down the tree and sat on the ground, trying to ward off a blather of big, wet licks. "Get off, ya silly puppy," I said, trying to push the big dog away, but he was having none of it. By the time I managed to calm him down, my face was wet and sticky.

"Samson! Off!" Kate said, and he backed away and sat down, smiling at me, his tongue hanging out.

"Are you okay?" Kate asked. "What are you doing here?"

"Matteo Rossi," I gasped. "He went that way." I waved a hand in the direction I thought I'd seen him disappear, though the more I thought about it, the more I wasn't so sure *which* direction he'd gone. "I think I need some water."

"I think you need to go home," Kate said. "You look sick as a dog, Harry."

"I'm fine," I said. "I just overdid it a bit, is all."

"I'll get some cruisers out searching for him. He can't get far that way. It gets pretty dense in there."

She offered me an arm and a disgusted look. "Don't breathe in my direction," she said. "I don't need to catch anything. Like I said, I have a vacation planned."

"Yeah, yeah," I blew her off, shaking my head. "I hope someone finds him before something happens to him."

"You think he killed the guy in the car?" Kate asked as we headed back toward the crime scene.

"I couldn't answer that even if I *thought* I knew the answer. Nothing makes any sense."

"You'll figure it out, Harry," she said as she put out a hand to help me over the fence.

I shook her hand off. "Thanks, Kate. I can manage."

"Hah!" she said. "Same old Harry Starke."

"Maybe," I said, not feeling much like talking. "I just need a drink. I haven't drunk enough water today. Dehydration is catching up to me."

"Okay, let me run in here and grab some water. Samson, you stay here with Harry."

I leaned against the wall, slowly getting my breath back.

Come on, Harry. Get a frickin' grip. I need to be able to work. I need to find Rossi.

Samson whined, looking up at me. I reached out and patted his head. "Good Boy," I said, and he sat down beside me, his haunches resting against my leg. Kate reappeared a moment later holding a large Styrofoam cup.

"Here," she said, shoving it into my hand. "Drink this. You look terrible, Harry."

"Thanks," I muttered as I sipped the cool liquid through the straw. "We have to do something about Rossi," I said between sips. "We don't want something to happen to him. I just don't fancy his chances out there on his own."

"I'll have a tri-state BOLO put out on him as soon as I get back to my car," Kate reassured me. "At least you know he's alive now. Unless…"

I shook my head. "Don't even go there. I know it was him. There's no doubt in my mind."

"Come on," Kate said. "I sent an officer in to get a list of the reservations at the hotel. Maybe we'll get a name."

"Rossi?" I said. "It won't be under that name."

"I know, but if I can get a list… I'll have it sent to Tim, okay?"

"Yeah," I said, still wondering if Matteo killed Waters, the man in the Ford Explorer. Or… if someone else killed him.

30

I SAT IN MY CAR FOR A GOOD HOUR, WATCHING AS DOC Sheddon worked the body and then had it removed to his forensic center three blocks from the police department on Amnicola. There was little more Mike Willis could do at the scene; it was probable the killer never left his vehicle.

I leaned my head back against the head rest with the window open and closed my eyes; Matteo Rossi's face etched into my brain. I had so many questions I wanted to ask him.

A few minutes later, I heard a tap on the hood of the car and opened my eyes to see Kate standing at the window.

"Looks like we're finishing up here," Kate said. "I issued the BOLO for Rossi ten minutes ago. How're you feeling?"

"I'm fine," I said. "How about you and I take a drive around the area? Maybe we'll get lucky. He can't have gone far."

"Sure," Kate said. "Your car or mine?"

"Mine, I think."

She nodded, had a word with a nearby uniformed officer, then she opened the rear door for Samson, climbed in the front, and put on her seat belt.

"You should probably eat something," she said. "You still look a little peaky."

"Nah. I'm fine," I said, firing up the engine. "Let's do this."

"Well, I'm not," she said. "How about we stop at Subway? We can go through the drive-through. Maybe you'll change your mind."

I nodded. "Sure," I said, "though I doubt it."

"So," she said, "which way did he go, d'you think?"

I nodded in the direction I thought Rossi had gone and said, "North. He was headed north." I put the car in drive, made a one-eighty in the parking lot, and turned north onto the two-lane road skirted by the interstate to the left and trees to the right. It was a guess, but it was all I had.

"It's a long shot," she said as I cruised along at twenty-five miles an hour.

"You got that right," I said.

I knew Rossi wouldn't be caught walking down the street. There were already patrol cars out looking for him, and my guess was that he was a survivor and knew what he was doing. The only way we were going to catch him was if he made a mistake.

"There's nowhere for him to hide," Kate said, her eyes on the thinly wooded area to our right. "There's little cover, and he'd be easily spotted. Maybe he caught a ride."

"Or maybe he stole another car," I said.

She nodded. "If he has, he could be halfway to Monteagle by now."

I shook my head at the thought, then said, "I wonder what the connection to Waters is? And how was he, Waters, connected to Isabella Rossi? And how come the kid doesn't look anything like a Rossi?"

"What... are you talking about? You sound like you're rambling."

"No, *no*." I shook my head and took a sip of water. "Rossi has a kid with his girlfriend, Catherine McCarthy. The only picture we have of the kid was when he was a baby. Amanda found a fairly recent one online. He looks nothing like Rossi."

"That's not that surprising," she replied. "Genetics can be a huge variable."

"Nah, you don't understand," I said. "Rossi has dark hair, dark eyes, and an olive complexion. Catherine has blue eyes and is a natural blonde. This kid has green eyes and blonde hair."

"Huh," Kate mused. "I don't see that as a big deal."

"The kid doesn't look anything like Rossi," I argued. "I don't think he's his."

"So what?" she asked. "Even if he isn't, it doesn't mean anything. So she sleeps around. So what?"

"True," I said, "but it's something, and right now... I dunno, Kate. Maybe I'm grasping at straws."

She didn't answer, her eyes on the trees as we cruised slowly onward.

"Why was Rossi on the run in the first place?" I said, more to myself than to Kate, "And who was it that killed Greg Mallen? Did Rossi kill Waters, and if so, why? What the hell is his motivation? People don't just pick up and disappear for no good reason. And why is Finn Doyle so bound and determined to find him? Somethings up, and I want to know what it is."

"And there are no warrants out for him?" Kate asked.

I shook my head. "He's squeaky clean, but he does have mob connections."

Kate turned her head to look at me. "Doyle hired you, so the Irish?"

I nodded. "Irish and Italian."

"Whew. Deadly," she said. "Playing both ends against the middle. No wonder he's on the run."

"You'd think so, wouldn't you?" I said. "But... Geez, Kate,

I wish I had the answer, but I don't. Nobody's talking, not Doyle, Rossi's mother, his girlfriend, and certainly not Enzo Massino. I'm beginning to think they're all in cahoots and it's us against them."

"Whoever *they* are," Kate said as I made a U-turn and headed back the way we'd come, the trees now on my side of the car.

"There'll be a drone with a heat-sensing camera out here soon," Kate said. "If he's out there, they'll find him, but I have a feeling he's long gone."

"Right," I muttered. "It is what it is, I guess... Maybe we should pay Carmen Rossi another visit. Don't you think it was kind of convenient she left the keys in the car? Something's off there. It could be she's helping him. Though it was Waters that took her car... Geez, what a convoluted mess."

I pulled in at the Subway. It was in the same strip mall as the Italian restaurant. She ordered a six-inch turkey and Swiss for her and a plain six-inch ham and cheese for Samson.

"You sure you don't want anything?" she asked.

I thought about it for a moment, then looked out at the young woman in the window and said, "I'll take a plain turkey and Swiss with lettuce and tomato, and we'll have two black coffees, please."

I paid for it, and the woman leaned out and handed me the bag of food. I handed it over to Kate, then pulled away from the drive-through, crossed the road into the motel parking lot, and parked next to Kate's unmarked cruiser.

"What's your plan for the rest of the day?" she asked as she unwrapped Samson's sandwich and handed it to him.

I heard strange noises from the back seat as he dug into it.

I looked at Kate. She grinned at me as she handed me my sandwich. "Don't worry about it, Harry. He'll clean up after himself, and I have some wipes in my car."

"I'm not worried about it," I said. "Jade makes a whole lot more mess than he will."

I took a bite of my sandwich and quickly realized it was just what I'd been needing. I was starving.

"So," Kate said between bites, "you going back to the office?"

"I hadn't really thought about it," I said. "Yeah. Back to the office, I guess. I need to see if Tim's found anything, and I have a feeling Doyle will come calling, sooner rather than later."

"Doyle," she said, "I can't believe you let him talk you into taking the case. What kind of man is he?"

"He's typical New York Irish, if there is such a thing, and he's full of… well, you know. He's big and he's tough, and his constant lighthearted demeanor hides a ruthless son of a bitch. I'd imagine he's not someone you'd want to cross."

"Geez, what were you thinking, Harry? That whole family is nothing but bad news. And after all the trouble we had with his mother, Morrigan. Sometimes I have to wonder about you; I really do."

"Yeah, but this isn't like that," I said, though deep down I knew it was. "Rossi is supposed to be Doyle's best friend, and…" The more I thought about it, the more ridiculous it seemed.

"Well, maybe Rossi is a killer for hire," she said and took a sip of her coffee.

"Maybe," I said with a shrug. The thought hadn't crossed my mind, but it made sense, at least a little.

"But I was hired to find him; nothing more, regardless of what he may or may not be, or the crimes he may or may not have committed. And that's what I'm going to do; nothing more."

"Ah, just the bare minimum, huh?"

"Hardly that," I said and rolled my eyes. "But I did *find*

Rossi, didn't I? We now know he's here in Chattanooga, so maybe I can call it quits, huh?"

She laughed and said, "If only it were that easy. I highly doubt a man like Doyle will let it go at that."

"Yeah, well, I don't intend to tell him I spotted him," I said with some thought. "I'd like to try and keep him out of the loop as much as possible." I took another bite of my sandwich, chewed thoughtfully for a moment, then swallowed it and said, "At least that's the plan... for now, anyway."

"I think you might be playing a dangerous game with a very dangerous man," Kate said after a few moments of silence. "I think you should proceed with caution, and maybe consider the consequences of leaving a man like Doyle out of the loop."

"You act like I can't handle him," I teased, grinning at her.

"In your condition? After what I saw an hour ago? You couldn't handle Jade. You want me to lend you Samson?"

Again, I grinned at her and said, "Methinks you underestimate me, Captain."

31

It was getting on for two o'clock when I walked into the outer office to find no one there. I could, however, hear voices somewhere toward the back.

I stepped around the front desk and followed the corridor to the break room, where I found Jacque, Heather, TJ and Tim drinking coffee and talking together.

"Harry. Nice of you to join us," Jacque said, a hint of sarcasm in her voice. "Where the hell have you been? It would be nice if you answered your phone."

I frowned, took my phone from my jacket pocket, looked at it and saw it was in silent mode. "Yeah, sorry about that," I said as I changed the setting.

"Are you all right? You look…" Heather's voice trailed off.

"Don't go there," I said. "I've had about all I can stand from Kate. Why is it all you women insist on trying to mother me?"

"They love you, Harry," TJ growled.

"Yeah, right," I said. "I have Amanda to handle that, so…" I trailed off, grinning at the group. "And I appreciate the concern, but I'm fine, really. I just overdid it, is all. I got into a chase with Matteo Rossi, and I lost."

"We heard," Jacque said, giving me a sympathetic smile. "Kate called me. We'll find him."

"But now we at least know he's alive," TJ said. "That's something."

"Kate said she put a BOLO out for him," Jacque said. "They'll find him."

"I wouldn't pin your hopes on that," I said. "Let's adjourn to the conference room. I need to sit down." And we did.

I pulled out a chair at the head of the table and sat down. "I think we're dealing with someone we've been underestimating. Kate suggested he might be a killer for hire, and he could be. One thing I know for sure is that he's a survivor who knows how to keep a low profile, so we mustn't let our guard down. And I'm thinking Doyle has an ulterior motive for finding him. Think about it. It makes no sense that he'd part with all that money just to find a missing friend. And why did Rossi disappear in the first place?"

"All of that is true," Jacque said, "but I think we're making some headway. Tim, why don't you tell Harry what you've found."

Tim took a deep breath, nodded, raked his fingers through his hair, and then pushed his glasses into place with a forefinger. "Well, for starters, Nick Waters is not an elusive guy. I dug deep into his connections, and it's no secret he works for Enzo Massino. Also, it appears that Waters was *much* closer to Rossi than anyone else."

"Really," I said, unable to hide my surprise. "Why have we not heard about him until today?"

"See the screen." Tim gestured to the screen on the wall connected to his computer via Bluetooth. It was showing a Facebook page. "This is Nick Waters."

Sure enough, I recognized the dead man. He was wearing a

suit and tie, his arm around none other than Matteo Rossi, and they were both smiling.

"How the hell did you find this? We scoured the internet for Rossi, and you're telling me he was right there on this guy's profile?"

"Yeah." Tim didn't appear at all fazed. "There's nothing on Rossi, and this didn't pop up until I searched for Waters. I think Waters was Rossi's best friend, not Doyle." He scrolled down the page, and picture after picture popped up of him and Rossi.

I shook my head. "But I thought he didn't want an internet presence, and then here we have this guy posting his mug all over his page? Come on, this is weird."

"Or maybe that's just what everyone wanted us to think," Heather said. "I think we should be considering that *maybe* someone—or a lot of someones—have been covering for Rossi."

"Geez, this is out of the park," I muttered, leaning back in my chair and folding my arms. "Who is this guy Waters?"

"A master hacker and private investigator," Tim said. "And he was one of the best, actually. I've known who he was on the dark web for years. I never knew he had ties to the mob, not until I did some digging into his personal life. It's no secret."

"Well, well, well." I chuckled. "Here we go. So, who shot him? And why?"

"I wouldn't think Rossi would have shot his best friend, not based on what we can see here," Tim said. "From what I can tell, they've been friends for years."

"What's the connection to Doyle, then?" I asked, trying to connect the dots in my head.

"None," Tim said. "At least, none that I can find. They work for different organizations. It also places Rossi smack dab in between the two different bosses. I don't know what that means for us, and it might be irrelevant, but I'm thinking Enzo hired Waters to find Rossi."

"That makes sense," Heather said, "but it doesn't explain why he was shot."

I slowly shook my head, staring up at the ceiling, thinking hard. "Well, Rossi was at the scene, but I don't think he shot him. Both Mike Willis and Doc think he was shot from the inside of a car. Rossi was on foot, which begs the question, how did he get there? And it was Waters that killed Greg Mallen."

"No," Heather answered. "It wasn't him. They picked that guy up just outside of Charleston."

"Right," Tim said and flipped to a picture of a blond-haired, scruffy-looking individual, and I had to admit, it did look like the man in the video footage. "I think Waters paid this guy to steal a car for him, and it went wrong. There's no doubt that it was Waters who made the switch between the Blazer and the Explorer, though."

I sighed and leaned forward. "But there's a significant lapse between the time we know the Explorer was taken out of Carmen's driveway and it showing up at the hotel."

"That's true," Heather said, "and he had to have been doing *something* during that time, but maybe we'll never know. We can't question Waters, can we?"

"But we *can* talk to Isabella Rossi," I said. "And I think that's something that needs to be done right away."

"You think there's a chance she might have hired someone to kill her son?" TJ asked. It was a question that came out of left field, but it had some merit to it. No one answered.

"Maybe she did," I said eventually. "It's impossible to know. But Rossi is on the run from someone. I just don't know who he's running from."

"Agreed," Heather chimed in. "And then there's another question we have to address. What about Doyle? Do we update him on what we've found? Should we tell him you've spotted Rossi? Or should we keep it to ourselves?"

"We'll keep it to ourselves, for now," I said. "It's a bit of a risk, but one we have to take until we can figure it out. What about the picture of the kid? Have you figured that out yet?"

"Oh," Tim mumbled. "No one has told him yet?"

"Told me *what?*" I said, frowning.

"We found a paternity test, but it's locked," Heather said quietly. "Catherine clearly wasn't sure who the father was. Tim is working to get around the encryption, but it's taking time."

I sighed. "So, now we know the child probably isn't Rossi's, but what does it matter? I don't see that it has any bearing on anything."

"Based on the fact that he's done a runner," TJ said, "I'd say he knows it isn't his. But you're right, Harry. It has no bearing on the case."

"Agreed," Jacque said. "You're right; both of you."

"Someone needs to go talk to Carmen Rossi," I said.

"She's going to be bombarded by Kate and her people, and maybe even the feds, so we need to be quick. And it doesn't need to be me."

"I'll go," Jacque said. "And I'll take Heather with me. She'll be more comfortable talking to two women."

I nodded. "Fine with me."

"What about you, Harry?" TJ said.

I drummed my fingertips on the table. "Someone needs to call Isabella Rossi. We need answers, and we don't have time to go jetting off to New York again."

"I can call her before we go visit with Carmen," Heather said. "I talked to her in New York, so she knows me."

I nodded. "Do it. Everyone else, get back to work."

They all stood and walked out into the hallway; all except Heather. The door closed and she took out her cell phone.

"You really think she wants her son dead?" I asked, frowning.

She shook her head. "I don't think so. I think she's trying to protect him."

I nodded but didn't reply.

She hesitated as she brought up the phone number. "I have something else to tell you, but you probably won't agree with it."

I sighed. "And what's that?"

"I think you need to go home and get some more rest, Harry. I've known you a long time, and it's easy to see you're still not up to scratch. You need rest."

"I'm fine," I said, a little irritated. "We have too much to do, and I don't need to be sitting at home sipping Gatorade."

Heather shook her head. "I just think you should take the afternoon off and come back tomorrow morning. I honestly don't think anything's going to happen before morning. You and I, we both have the same gut feeling that Rossi isn't going down easy."

I grimaced. "Okay. Fine. Now make the call."

32

Isabella Rossi picked up on the second ring. "I was wondering when I'd hear from you again." Her tone was disinterested, with a hint of what sounded a little like annoyance.

"What do you know about a man named Nick Waters?" Heather asked, taking the lead. I'd already decided to speak only if necessary. Heather had already built a little rapport with Isabella.

"Nick Waters?" Isabella echoed. "Not familiar."

I frowned. I wasn't expecting her to play stupid. I turned to Heather, who appeared equally surprised. She shrugged and then pressed on.

"With all due respect, Mrs. Rossi, we know that's not true. His phone records tell a different story. He's been calling you regularly."

I heard a heavy sigh, then she said, "Yes. Okay. I know him. He works for Enzo. He was supposed to be looking for my son, and he was making good progress. So, why are you asking about him? He hasn't been arrested, has he?"

Heather pursed her lips, looked at me, raised her eyebrows and then delivered the news. "I'm afraid he's dead, Mrs. Rossi.

He was killed this morning." There was a long moment of silence, and then Heather said, "Mrs. Rossi?"

"Sorry, um…" She sounded distraught, as if on the verge of tears. "I can't believe it… He was… He was a good friend of Matty's, and I… I really thought he was going to find him."

I almost told her that I put eyes on her son but chose to hold back. The fact that she wasn't forthcoming about her connection to Nick Waters had hit a nerve, and I wasn't sure if we could trust her or not. I mean, why would she want to hide her connection with Waters if he was merely trying to find Matteo?

"When did you last hear from him?" Heather asked.

"Last night, around ten," Isabella replied. "He said he was close."

"That's all he said?" Heather asked.

"I said so, didn't I?" she snapped, then seemed to regret it. "I can't believe he's dead. He was a good man."

"D'you have any idea who killed him, Isabella?" Heather asked.

The hardness returned to her voice, and her reaction was surprising.

"Whoever is hunting Matty, that's who," she snapped. "I'm sure by now you people know he's on the run. Nick figured that out four days ago, and he trailed him all the way to Tennessee. I don't even know why he'd be in Tennessee."

"He has an aunt here," Heather said quietly. "Carmen."

"Hah, she's hardly an aunt," Isabella spat out. "She's a distant acquaintance at best."

"But Nick was found in her car." I looked at Heather. Her expression was hard to read, but I hoped she'd be careful not to reveal any more details than she had to. Once again, the question of how much we could trust Isabella Rossi reared its ugly head. She had not been too forthcoming in the past, though I'd put that down to not being a fan of Finn Doyle, or maybe even private detectives in general.

"I don't have an answer for you," Isabella said curtly. "And I need to get going. I'm visiting my son, my *other* son." With that, the line clicked, ending the call.

I shook my head. "I don't like it one bit."

"Something is off," Heather agreed. "I don't know what it is, but somebody knows a lot more than they're letting on. I mean, take Isabella's story about the aunt living here in Tennessee. It almost felt forced."

"Or she just doesn't want to talk to us," I said. "And she also could've been in shock from the news of Waters' death. You did kind of drop it on her."

"Hah!" Heather sighed. "Maybe Carmen Rossi will be able to tell us more. Of course, if they're in communication... She and Isabella."

"We'll just have to wait and see," I said. "At this point, there's no telling what's going to happen next, and I can't help but wonder why Matteo ran when I tried to talk to him."

"As you say, Harry. We'll just have to wait and see, but I'm thinking there's still a lot more to this that we have to uncover."

Heather picked up her phone and put it back in her pocket, then she pushed back from the table and stood up.

"You need to go home, Harry. I'll keep you updated as the evening progresses. Get some rest. You still look like a ghost."

"I'll be fine," I said as I stood up, feeling slightly dizzy. It lasted but a few moments, and I chalked it up to dehydration, figuring I'd stop somewhere on the way home to grab a bottle of Gatorade. "But I think I'll take you up on it. Keep me in the loop, Heather. I'll see you in the morning."

I told Jacque what I planned to do, then left the office and went to my car, checking my surroundings as I did so.

I stood for a moment with my hand on the door handle,

staring unseeing at the busy Riverfront Parkway, wondering if Matteo Rossi had high-tailed it out of town or if he was still lurking somewhere in the city. One question still begged to be answered: *What—or who—is he running from?*

In my mind, I listed the possibilities, most of them mob related. But at the back of it all was the story we'd been told of him being overtly paranoid about the government. Was it just another ruse to cover his tracks? Or was it something else?

In the end, I sighed, shook my head, opened the door and slid in behind the wheel where I sat for another moment, the wheels spinning inside my head. Finally, I pulled out onto the Parkway, turned left onto MLK, then right on Broad, and from there to the split and headed on up the mountain toward home, making a quick stop at a convenience store along the way, the last one just before the split.

I grabbed three bottles of Gatorade Zeros, paid for them, had the clerk double bag them, and then headed back out to my car, paying little attention to my surroundings, which wasn't like me and probably wouldn't have happened had I not still been recovering from the flu.

Anyway, it was a *big* mistake.

As I reached for the door handle, there was a flash of bright light and pain seared through the back of my skull. I staggered sideways and then went down, my vision darkening. Whoever had hit me had come from out of nowhere. I tried to spin around but was dealt another stunning blow to the side of my head.

At that point, I almost blacked out, but somehow I managed to hang on. I swung the bag of drinks at the now shadowy figure, but I missed, and as I spun, I was dealt a third blow, this time to my temple. I felt my consciousness beginning to slip away.

Who is doing this? The question reverberated through my brain as I took another hit to the ribs. I raised my arms to block yet another blow to my head, knowing that another good solid hit there would put me under and possibly even kill me, and I couldn't help but wonder if that was my assailant's intent.

I winced with every hit, my arms over my head, my eyes closed. My instincts were screaming for me to fight back, but to remove my arms from around my head meant exposing myself.

"This'll show you," I heard a muffled voice say. I couldn't quite make it out in the moment, but on thinking about it later, it sounded almost foreign.

I forced a deep breath as another shot hit me in the hip. My ears were ringing. My head was spinning. But through it all, I knew I was in deep trouble and had to do something—and fast.

In a moment of clarity, I reached up, grabbed the car door handle, and with a burst of adrenaline, I swung the bag of drinks with every ounce of strength I had left, and it connected.

A fractured cry came from the figure, a figure I couldn't quite see, thanks to the direct hit to my occipital nerve in the back of my head from the first blow. It didn't matter, however. It was all the time I needed to clamber into the car and lock the doors. How I did it, I'm still not sure. I remember hitting the lock button and hearing them click into place. And all I could do was sit there, my head spinning, desperately wanting to see who it was that had attacked me.

I blinked several times, trying to ward off the blackness that was threatening to overtake me. The ringing in my ears morphed into buzzing. I couldn't hear anything. I hung onto the steering wheel, trying to breathe through the symptoms of what I knew to be a concussion.

Then, somehow, I managed to turn my head enough to peer out of the driver's side window, half expecting to see Rossi or maybe someone about to shoot me through the window.

But that's not what I saw. What I saw was a petite figure and a pair of emerald-green eyes, and I remember thinking I was dreaming. My head was pounding, my vision blurry, and the green eyes were gone in a matter of seconds, leaving me staring at... nothing.

I took a deep, shuddering breath, knowing I was in big trouble and that I needed to call someone before I blacked out completely. I remember struggling to get my cell phone out of my jeans pocket, growing groggier by the second.

"Come on, Harry," I muttered, or at least, I thought I did. Maybe my consciousness was playing tricks on me. I don't know. I do know I managed to jerk the phone from my pocket and fumble with it just before I slid away into oblivion.

33

Tap, tap, tap...

I groaned, searing pain shooting through the back of my head. I squeezed my eyes tightly together, wishing the noise would stop.

Tap, tap, tap, tap.

It sounded like someone was banging on the window with a rock.

"Harry!" a muffled voice shouted. *Tap, tap, tap.*

"Make it stop," I mumbled under my breath, my neck aching with every little movement. My entire body felt as if it had been put through a rock crusher, and for a moment, I thought maybe I'd driven the car off the side of the mountain...

But then memory replaced fantasy, and I jerked my head upward, instantly regretting it, seeing brilliant white stars. I grimaced, turned my head a little and was relieved to see the face peering into the car. I ran my fingers through my hair, feeling the dried blood caked over the back of my head. I took a deep, shuddering breath that sent spears of intense pain ratcheting through my brain and body, but somehow I managed to reach sideways and lower the window.

DUPLICITY

"What the hell happened to you?" Kate said, exasperated, her eyes wide. "Amanda called me, saying you never made it home and that she was worried."

"What time is it?" I muttered, my mouth feeling as if it was full of cotton balls.

"It's almost five o'clock," she said, her voice tense. "What happened? You get in a fight? Fall? If I hadn't stumbled across your car here... Geez, Harry. I was about to call in search and rescue."

I gave her a weak smile. "Probably overkill."

"Amanda wouldn't think so," Kate said. "Now tell me what happened?"

"Some woman beat the daylights out of me," I answered, gently rubbing my forehead.

"A *woman?*" Kate shook her head. "You've got to be kidding me. You look like you got into an altercation with a pack of bears."

"It was a woman," I said. "I know it was. Whoever it was, was too small to be a man... And anyway, I saw her face." Though I couldn't remember a single detail other than her eyes.

Kate shook her head. "Geez, Harry. You look sick as a dog. Talk about getting hit when you're already down. We need to take you to the hospital."

"No, I just need to go home," I said, not feeling up to a trip to the hospital. "I'll be as well off at home as I would at the hospital."

"Uh-uh," she said, shaking her head. "I talked to Heather. She said it was almost two when you left her. You've been unconscious for almost three hours, and you think you *don't* need to see a doctor?" Kate stared through the window at me. "Come on, Harry. You at least need to get checked out."

I shook my head, ignoring the pain every little movement

caused. "I really just want to get home. If I was going to die, it would've happened already."

Kate didn't find the attempt at humor the least bit funny. "I'll drive you."

"I'll drive myself. You follow me. I don't want to leave my car here."

"No," she argued. "That's not a good idea."

"What a shame. I'll write it down so I don't forget," I quipped, reaching down and starting the engine. "I'll be fine, Kate. It's just a few minutes."

She stared at me for a few moments and then sighed. "Fine. But I'm following you."

"Got it." I gave her a weak thumbs-up and smiled. "Just try to keep up, Gazzara."

She rolled her eyes, tapping my car door before turning to her car parked right next to mine.

As I waited for her to get in, I could see Samson eyeing me balefully through the open window.

Geez, even he knows I shouldn't be driving, I thought. *But I'd rather wait it out at home than sit in a hospital.*

It took a little more than ten minutes to drive home, my head throbbing but my vision clear. As soon as I pulled into the garage, Amanda was there, waiting for me. Kate had called her.

"Thank you, Kate," Amanda said. Then she turned to me as I hauled my aching body out of the car and said, "What the hell happened to you?"

"Got beat up... by a girl, would you believe?" I laughed as I said it, and it hurt like hell. "I think she must have used a baseball bat... or something."

"I don't know if that's true," Kate said, leaning out of the driver's side window. "But I'm going to head back down there and see what I can find out. I'm sure the convenience store has security cameras, but you never know. We might get lucky. I'll be back. I need to talk to you, Harry." She nodded to us and then rolled up her window and drove away.

Me? I leaned against the car door and took a moment, breathing hard, pain wracking my body.

"Are you all right, Harry?" Amanda asked, taking my arm. "I think maybe I should take you to the ER."

I shook my head, and together we walked slowly into the house.

"I just need to sit down," I said. "I don't know who did it, but I'm pretty damn sure it has something to do with this Rossi case."

"But you don't *know* that," Amanda said as she led me to the couch. "I think you need a drink. Take some deep breaths while I fetch you a glass of Laphroaig."

"Ah, yes," I said. "Good thinking. Whisky is always the best medicine." I was teasing, but she obviously didn't find it funny because she pursed her lips, turned away and disappeared into the kitchen. I leaned back against the couch and closed my eyes. Experience told me I had a concussion, but I wasn't sure how severe it was.

Maybe it was random, I thought as I touched the sore spot on the back of my head. *Or someone with a grudge. Whoever it was must have followed me. But why?*

"Did they steal your wallet?" Amanda's voice broke my thoughts, and I looked up at her as she held out the glass.

"No," I said, patting my pocket just to make sure. "I don't think they had robbery in mind. I think they just wanted to beat me to a bloody pulp."

She sat down in the armchair opposite me, crossed her legs, clasped her hands together in her lap, frowned at me and said, "And you think it was a woman? Seriously?" She looked at me skeptically.

"I do." I gave her a weary look. "I know what it sounds like, but I haven't been on my game today. I saw Rossi and chased him, but..."

"Yes. So I heard. Kate told me about what happened this morning." Amanda frowned. "You should've called. I would've come and picked you up, then this wouldn't have happened."

I shook my head. "Nah," I replied. "Woulda, coulda, shoulda. That kind of thinking is a waste of time. We can't predict the unpredictable. Let it go. I need to rest up so I can get back to it. I'm expecting Doyle to show his face soon."

Amanda sighed. "Maybe you and Kate should team up. I know she has the case... the murder in the hotel parking lot this morning. So, in a roundabout way, she's already involved in your case."

I nodded. "If it would make you feel better, I'll talk to her about it. I also need to talk to the team—"

"I called Jacque when you didn't show up," Amanda said. "And I texted her after Kate let me know she'd found you... Harry, you look awful. Are you sure you're okay?" Her voice wavered. "I never know with you." A tear rolled down her cheek. She batted it away with her hand.

"I'm fine, sweetheart," I said, hoping to reassure her. "If I hadn't already been weakened by that damn stomach bug, I wouldn't have gotten knocked down. I was just... I got caught on an off day."

She frowned at me. "You take too many chances, Harry. One of these days—"

"Yeah, I know. I'm sorry." I gave her a smile. I downed what was left of the whisky and rested my head against the cushion on the back of the couch. I closed my eyes, thinking it was a miracle I'd managed to get into the car. Would she have killed me? Or was she sending me a message? *What was it she'd said? This'll show you... Something like that. What the hell did she mean? Show me... what?*

"I'm going to make you something to eat," Amanda said, standing up. "I know you might not feel up to it, but you need something inside you."

I nodded. "Good idea. Hopefully, there'll be no more excitement. At least, not tonight."

She shook her head and grimaced, and my gut knotted.

That's not a good sign.

34

I finally dozed off after an uneasy bowl of wild rice chicken soup and crackers. Amanda promised to wake me up once an hour to ensure the head trauma wasn't so severe I'd fall asleep and never wake up. However, it *wasn't* Amanda that woke me up at three-thirty in the morning.

It was the *doorbell.*

"What the hell?" I muttered as I pulled back the covers. I glanced at Amanda. She was still sleeping. The doorbell ringing shifted to knocking, and I grabbed my gun on the way to the front door. My headache had receded to a mere dull ache.

I peered through the peephole and my jaw dropped.

Matteo Rossi.

And he was covered in blood.

I swallowed hard, flipped on the porch light and opened the door. He looked terrified.

"Mr. Starke?" Rossi choked out. Then, as he looked at me, his eyes widened. "You're the guy who chased me today." He sounded confused. "I had no idea it was you. Please. I need help. My mother said I could come to you."

"Come on in, Matteo." I opened the door further and stood

aside to let him in, then I closed the door, locked it and set the chain.

I took him through to the kitchen and sat him down. "Wait here. I'll be right back. I'm going to get dressed."

Rossi nodded and then glanced around the kitchen.

I went back to the bedroom and quickly dressed in jeans and a T-shirt. Then, I woke Amanda and said, "I have to go. Rossi's here, and I need to take him to the police department."

"What?" Amanda rolled over, her voice groggy. "What do you mean?"

"Our missing person is downstairs, in the kitchen, covered in blood. I need to get him to Kate." I kept my voice low, trying not to act as concerned as I actually felt. I wasn't happy about the idea of hauling Rossi anywhere, but I didn't see that I had a choice. "Call Maria and see if she can come over to be with you and Jade. If you can't get ahold of her, call Jacque."

She nodded. "Please call for backup for you, too," Amanda said, reaching out and squeezing my hand. "Please."

I nodded, giving her a smile I didn't feel, then went to the bathroom where I called Kate. She didn't pick up, so I texted her, and just as I tapped send, my phone rang.

I looked at the screen. *Heather?*

"Odd timing," I said.

"Yeah, I'm on my way to your house. I just got a phone call from Isabella Rossi. She said Matteo was on his way to you. Apparently, he's giving it up."

"He's already here," I replied.

"Don't do anything," she said. "I heard what happened to you. Wait for me to get there. We don't know anything about Rossi. And we don't know who attacked you. Stay put. I'm ten minutes out."

"You got it," I said. "Hold on. I left him in the kitchen. He looked scared to death, and he's covered in blood."

"Oh geez," Heather muttered. "What have we gotten ourselves into?"

"I have no idea," I replied. "I'll see you when you get here." I hung up the phone, thought for a moment and then went back downstairs to the kitchen where Rossi was still sitting at the table, head down, his hands in his lap.

He looked up at me. "Are we going now? Can we go? I'm sure they know where you live."

"Do you have any weapons on you?" I asked quietly.

He shook his head. "No, no, I don't. I *did,* but I don't anymore."

"What happened?" I said, gesturing to his bloody shirt.

"I don't want to talk about it until we're somewhere safe," Rossi said, glancing around us. "And I don't understand why we're still here. Can we go now?"

"Who is after you?" I asked.

"Get me somewhere safe and I'll talk." Matteo's voice sharpened. "They're everywhere, and for all I know, they're listening. Right here."

He really is quite paranoid, I thought. But my gut was telling me he had good reason, but at the same time, I knew from experience that a paranoid, panicky man was also the most unpredictable—and the most dangerous.

"No one is listening to us here," I assured him. "But we can wait. I don't mind. I'm waiting for backup."

"You think I'm crazy, don't you?" He wiped his face with the back of his hand. "I had to leave everything," he said. "I had to just run like hell."

"I don't think you're crazy," I said easily. "But I do have a lot of questions for you." I eyed the blood on his shirt once more.

"I'll answer them. I swear. I just need to be somewhere safe."

"I can take care of that," I said as I heard a knock at the door.

So did Rossi, and he leapt to his feet and ran to the back door. Fortunately, it was locked. He turned around, wide eyes with terror, and stared at me. "They're here. What do we do?"

"We calm down," I said. "It's my backup."

I didn't know if it was or if it wasn't, but I needed him not to do anything stupid.

Rossi hesitated. "The feds?"

"No." I laughed. "Heather is no fed. She just drives a Tahoe. Come on. You can ride up front."

"Why aren't you driving us?" Rossi still lingered by the back door. "That your wife?" He was looking behind me.

I looked around to see Amanda standing behind me, her arms folded.

"Yes. Her name's Amanda."

He looked at her for a moment, then obviously still unsure, said, "Hi, Mrs. Starke. I'm Matteo. I'm sorry…" He trailed off.

"Hello, Matteo," Amanda said, then to me, "Maria's on her way. Harry—"

"It's okay," I said. "Heather's here. We need to go."

"Why can't you take me?" Matteo asked again.

"I'm not fit to drive," I said. "I was attacked yesterday afternoon, and I may have a concussion. Come on."

Reluctantly, he followed me to the front door but stood back as I opened it.

I turned, grabbed his arm, and together we followed Heather back to her SUV. He climbed into the front passenger seat. I eased myself slowly into the back seat on the driver's side, giving myself the best angle to observe Rossi as he pulled on his seat belt.

For all the searching we'd done, in the end, the man came to us.

But something about it just didn't sit right with me, and I had to wonder what the hell was going on.

However, Rossi seemed to be of sound mind, at least from what I could tell. I had no doubt he was seriously paranoid, and as Heather reversed out of my driveway, he began twisting this way and that, trying to see in every direction.

Heather turned around to face the rear as she reversed the SUV and gave me a concerned look.

I merely shrugged. As much as I should've been disturbed by what I'd seen of Rossi so far, I just... wasn't. What I was interested in was knowing what the hell had happened to him and who he thought was after him. I needed to know if it was his paranoia telling him the government was out to get him, or a credible fear.

"I'm Heather," she said and gave him a half-smile as she started down the mountain. "I spoke with your mom when we were in New York. She seemed nice."

I almost laughed at the statement, but however cheesy it was... it worked. In only a matter of minutes, Heather had Rossi calmed down, somewhat.

"Yeah, she's nice for an Italian lady." He chuckled, shaking his head. "And Lord knows I've put her through the wringer this year." His New York accent was prominent, almost as prominent as the sadness etched in his expression.

"She's really worried about you," Heather said as she turned onto Scenic Highway. "What was it like growing up with her?"

"Uh, fine, I guess." He shrugged. "I had a good childhood. It just sucks I had to blow it as an adult." He leaned against the door panel and then rested his forehead against his palm. He looked totally exhausted, and I couldn't help but feel a little sympathy for him.

But he was still being cagey with his answers, and I wasn't sure if it was because he wasn't sure if he could trust us or if there was something more sinister going on. I didn't like not knowing, but I was letting Heather take the lead, and she seemed to be doing a good job of it.

"What about your brother?" she asked. "Micah, isn't it? Are you close to him?" Heather asked. "Are you two close?"

"Yeah, sure. I guess."

"And your aunt Carmen?" Heather slipped it in so gracefully, and I realized she probably knew a lot more about said Carmen than I did. I hadn't checked my email since the incident in the parking lot of the convenience store, and I figured there'd probably been developments in the Carmen Rossi department that I didn't know about.

"I'm not close to her," Rossi answered. "But I know her well enough that I thought she'd help me out once I got here. But it didn't work out that way."

Unable to stay quiet any longer, I butted in and said, "Did you steal her car, Matteo?"

Rossi turned to look back at me. "No!" he replied. "Why would I steal a car from someone I know? That's never a good idea. I called once I made it to Chattanooga, but she didn't want to know; she told me not to call her again and hung up."

"But someone stole her car," I said, pushing him a little more. "A black Ford Explorer."

Something shifted in Rossi's face, but he shook his head. "Yeah? Well, I don't know."

"So, what happened?" Heather asked, pointing to his shirt. "It's probably better for us to know now, before we get where we're going."

Rossi eyed us each in turn, with a strange expression on his face, then said, "I killed someone."

35

The bluntness left Heather and I silent for a few moments, then, wanting to keep him talking, I picked up the conversation and said, "Who did you kill, Matteo?"

"Bethany Rodriguez," Rossi answered, his lips curled downward. "She was a contract hitman, well, woman. She worked for anyone who'd hire her. She was a total bitch, small but efficient."

That struck a nerve with me. "Go on," I said, frowning. "Can you describe her?"

"Huh?" Rossi frowned, wrinkled his forehead and said, "Yeah, I guess. Brown hair, small, skinny, kinda nondescript... except that she had these real bright green eyes. Her father was Hispanic, but her mother was Irish. She was Irish. She came here from the old country some six or seven years ago, I think."

So that's who it was, I thought. *I got lucky; lucky she didn't beat me to death.*

"And she was after you, right?" Heather turned her head to look at him.

"Yeah, and I'm sure she won't be the last."

"Why?" I said. "What do you mean?"

"They'll just keep sending more people after me until the job is done. They want me gone, Mr. Starke. The woman found me, broke into my hotel room, and then tried to kill me. Had I not been awake, I would've been dead."

Before I could say anything else to him, my phone began to ring. Strange for the time of night—early morning.

It was Kate.

"Hold on a second," I said, holding up a finger to Heather and Rossi. "I need to take this." I sat back in the seat and took the call. "Hey, Kate."

"Funny you called," she began. "I'm back at that hotel. You know, the one where we found Waters?"

"Really?" I couldn't hide my surprise. "At this time of night? Were you able to get some security footage?"

"Some, not much," she said. "But I was able to get security footage from the convenience store, and we were able to identify the person who attacked you—"

"Bethany Rodriguez," I said, interrupting her,

"Yes, Bethany Rodriguez... How do you know that? Never mind that for now. She's dead, which is why I'm here. She had a room next to someone called Matt Ross. I don't think it's much of a leap to figure that one out. Anyway, someone heard a ruckus in the next room and called the manager. He found the body."

I grimaced. "I think I can help you with that." I eyed Rossi, sitting in the front seat. "Meet me at the station?"

"Vague answer. Must be the concussion."

"Or the company," I answered her, hoping she would catch on.

"You want to explain that?" she asked testily.

"Long story." I sighed. "Better if you just meet me at the station."

"Got it. Mike and Doc are both here, but I'll try to wrap it up here as quick as I can and meet you there. I'll call in and let them know to give you a room."

"Thanks—"

"Oh, one more thing, Harry," Kate interrupted me before I could hang up. "If you're in the company of the person who's responsible for this... be careful. This is one messy scene. I've never seen a table lamp used with such... force."

I shuddered. "Okay," I replied. "You can bring me up to speed when you get here."

"Yep. Ask 'em to make some fresh coffee. See you soon."

"You got it," I said and hung up.

I looked at the man in the front seat. *A table lamp? Are you kidding me? A contract killer? What the hell? And if it was self-defense, why did he take off running? First Waters and then this Rodriguez woman. Who the hell is after him? Doyle?* I was trying to piece it all together, but something wasn't making any sense.

However, I didn't want to go digging in too deep until we made it to the police station. The last thing I needed was to further aggravate Rossi. He was already on the edge, and I didn't want him barreling out of the moving vehicle.

"How about it, Matteo?" Heather said, glancing at Rossi. "Anything else you want to tell us?"

Rossi took a deep breath and shook his head. "I'm dead either way, so no."

"What about your son?" she asked. "Is there anything you want to pass along to your family?"

Rossi burst into an eerie laughter. "My son? Have you seen the kid? He's not mine. Cat was cheating the whole time we were together. I was a scapegoat, and I just let her do it because what else was I supposed to do? She named the kid after me and then had the guts to try to convince me he was mine."

"Are you sure he's not yours?" Heather asked without looking at him. "Did you take a paternity test?"

"Yeah, we did. And the results were negative. He's not mine." He shifted his gaze to the window and shook his head. "Waste of a life. That's what I am."

"No one is a waste of a life," Heather said quietly. "You're still young. You have your whole life ahead of you."

"Yeah?" He turned to her and rolled his eyes. "A life behind bars. That's some kind of future to look forward to."

"Maybe not if you tell us what happened," Heather said, and I kneed the back of her seat. I wasn't sure I wanted to continue the interview in the car. Better it was done in an interview room where it would be recorded, not barreling down the highway at eighty miles per hour.

"There's not much to tell," Rossi muttered. "You know we're being followed, right?" He nodded to the side mirror. "They've been tailing us since we started down the mountain, Mr. Starke."

I spun around in the seat, surprised to see someone tailing us, and they were close; close enough for me to see the driver. By then we were on Georgia, under the bright lights of downtown, heading for Riverside Drive, and I was surprised to see it was Finn Doyle.

"I think Mr. Doyle found us," I said.

Everything about Rossi's demeanor changed. "We need to go. *Now!*"

"It's okay. He's our client," I said, and I sent Kate a text asking her for backup.

"Yeah, and he's trying to kill me," Rossi yelled. "My mom didn't tell me it was *you* who was working for him! I gotta get outta here." He grabbed the door handle. Heather tapped the door lock button and sped up.

"Calm down, Matteo," I said. "We're on your side. Yes, he

might've hired us, but we're not going to hand you over to him. Just tell us what's going on."

"You don't understand," he practically whined. "You have no idea how much that man hates me."

"Well, why don't you enlighten us," I said, thinking we'd finally get to the bottom of what was really going on. "Why don't you—"

I was interrupted by an almighty thump as Doyle's SUV rammed into the back of Heather's and we were sent careening forward.

"Son of a bitch," Heather muttered as she made a hard right onto McCallie, her foot to the floor as she hurtled through the red light.

"Nice," Rossi commented dryly, hanging onto the handle over the window.

"Yeah, but let's try to get to the station in one piece," I said, trying to keep my head from spinning.

"Well, hang on. Doyle's back on our tail again," Heather yelled, fighting the wheel as she made a hard left onto Houston and hurtled through one stop sign and then another, the big car rocking as she slammed her foot down hard on the gas pedal, heading for Riverside. "Call him off, Harry. Do something. Call him. Tell him to follow us to the station where we can talk it over."

"I can try," I said. I scrolled through my contacts to Doyle's number and hit call, hoping like hell Kate had seen my message for backup. I put the phone to my ear, waiting for it to connect.

"Mr. Starke," Doyle growled. "Will ya pull the hell over before ya get hurt?"

"Why the hell did you just rear-end us," I growled back at him. "You could've called before you started trying to wreck us."

"And you could've called to let me know you found Rossi."

"Yes, I found him, and he has a lot of explaining to do. Someone tried to kill me, and I want to know why. Now back off and follow us to the police department."

"And I'd like for you to do the job I hired you to do," he said, his voice somehow menacing and cordial at the same time.

"I think we might owe you a refund," I told him as we approached Riverside.

Heather blew through two sets of lights and made a hard right onto Riverside, tires squealing.

"Back off, Doyle," I said. "We're done—" My phone pinged in my ear. I glanced at the screen.

I have you on Riverside. Backup on the way. I'll be there in ten.

I sighed and then put the phone back to my ear. "Just back off, Finn. We can work it out, okay?"

"You're making a big mistake, Harry, so y'are. You don't know what you're doing. He's a bad guy. He killed my pal, Patrick O'Connor. He's got to go."

"I think there's more to the story," I said, "and I want to hear it." It was a shot in the dark, but after what had happened to me at the convenience store, the case had moved from business to personal. Not to mention that Doyle had given me a bad feeling right from the beginning. "Follow us to the police station and we can talk."

"I'm not going to no police station, Harry," he snapped. "You should know better than that. We need to end this right now."

"Now listen—" But he hung up before I could finish. "Damn it!" I dropped the phone on the seat beside me. "We're in for it. He's not backing down."

Heather shook her head. "Where's our backup?" she asked as she blew through the lights at Wilcox Boulevard.

"On its way." I glanced out the rear window. The headlights were incoming faster than ever.

"Put your foot down, Heather," I snapped. "I think he's trying to—"

There was another almighty thump as the SUV took a *hard* hit. The car fishtailed as Heather fought to maintain control. She slammed her foot down, the big car surged forward, and I slammed back against the seat.

BAM! He hit us again. Again, Heather managed to keep control.

We bore left onto Amnicola, accelerating hard. I figured we were doing at least eighty when—BAM!—he hit us again on our left rear fender. Again, Heather fought the wheel, but this time the big car went into a spin, out of control, she managed to correct it, but by then we were off the road. The big vehicle bounced twice, slewed to the right and hit a light pole. We were four blocks from the station.

36

"Stay where you are, Rossi," I shouted, grabbing his shirt collar as he hit the door lock button and grabbed the door handle.

"Doyle will kill me," Rossi shouted as he strained against my hold, shoving the door open with his foot. The night breeze rushed into the cab of the car, and much to my relief, I heard sirens.

"Shut the door, Rossi!" Heather shouted. "We're going to be in a hell of..." She trailed off as a figure appeared in the opening, leaving us all staring down the barrel of a sawed-off Winchester 12-gauge shotgun.

"Now, come on, Doyle," I urged. "You don't want this. You *really* don't want to do this. It's not going to go well for you."

"Oh, *everything* works out just foine for me, Mr. Starke," Doyle said with a cackle. Rossi jerked backward, his hands over his face. "And yous don't owe me a t'ing. See, this *foine* young man here had something that I wanted for meself, and now I got it. Rossi, here... Well, he's just in the way."

"I've *never* stood in your way, Finn," Rossi shot back at him. "You wanted Catherine, and you got her. You knocked her up, and I've never made a fuss about it. *You* were the one who wouldn't step up to the plate and be there for him—"

"She named *my* frickin' son after *you*, y'bastard." Doyle growled, shoving the barrel of the gun into Rossi's face. "Y'tink you were there for her, but you *never* were. You were too wrapped up in your weird theories about the government and—"

"And what does that have to do with anything?" Rossi cut him off. "I thought you and I were *friends,* Finn. You killed Nicky!"

Heather and I exchanged glances, and for maybe the first time in my life, I felt like just another onlooker. Or maybe I was watching a bad movie. I glanced out of the back window, relieved to see Kate, Samson, and a half dozen uniformed officers approaching the car, weapons drawn.

"Put the gun down, Mr. Doyle," Kate shouted. The command was followed by a choppy bark from Samson, equally demanding.

"With all due respect, Captain," Doyle said when he turned to look at her, "I don't t'ink I will."

And it was then that Heather lunged across Rossi, grabbed the barrel of the shotgun with both hands, and ripped it from Doyle's grasp. She whipped it round and pointed it at him. It was the smoothest move I'd seen in a long time, since before Bob Ryan went back to working with the feds.

I watched as Doyle's demeanor changed from triumph to defeat.

Slowly, he raised his hands and dropped to his knees. Two of the uniformed officers pounced and cuffed him, then Rossi.

I climbed out of the car, as did Heather, though she had to crawl across and exit through the passenger door.

"Either of you hurt?" Kate said.

I looked at Heather. She shook her head, though she was

rubbing her left arm. I figured maybe she impacted the driver's side door, but I shook my head and told her no.

"That's a relief," Kate said. "Then I'll give you a ride to the station. I'll have the guys get these two set up in rooms for you, my treat. I'll let you have the first go, but I'm going to be there. Rossi is all over that murder back at the hotel."

"What about Nick Waters?" I asked. My back had started to twinge, but I brushed it off as just another in a long line of discomforts I'd endured since Finn Doyle first walked into my office.

"All I know is he's dead," Kate said as we climbed into her vehicle. Heather sat in the back with Samson, who seemed delighted to meet a new friend. "We're still trying to piece that one together, but the Charleston PD confirmed they've picked up a suspect for Mallen's murder."

"Oh?" I raised my brow.

"Yup. It seems someone hired a local car thief to steal a car from the dealership, and he was to meet his client at a gas station two streets over. The gas station security footage proved it, and the handover was made to none other than Nick Waters. Though I don't think he knew his thief had killed Mallen, not that it would have made a difference."

I nodded, glancing back at Heather, who was shaking her head. "And so, we've got what?" she asked. "Three murders in connection to this goose chase?"

"Something like that." Kate chuckled. "Harry was lucky he wasn't number four, I think. I told you we caught Rodriguez on camera assaulting you, right?"

I nodded.

"What I didn't tell you," she continued, "is that she had a reservation at the hotel."

"Clever." I didn't bother to hide the sarcasm from my tone. "But what about Nick Waters? Rossi said that Doyle killed him.

What was he doing? And did you hear that exchange we just had with Doyle? Could it be possible that this whole mess is over a paternity dispute?"

"That would be... daytime soap opera worthy," Kate said.

"Doyle also said something about a Patrick O'Connor..." My voice trailed off. "Do you know anything about that? He said Rossi killed him."

"Who knows?" Kate laughed. It was a dry laugh, unamused. "At this point, I think I might believe anything. We're going to have to sit down and grill these men. Someone has the answers."

"We know that Rossi killed Rodriguez," I said. "So, we can hold him on that, though I do think it was self-defense. Rossi said Rodriguez was a contract killer, and having experienced her, I think he might be telling the truth. Doyle, though, is going to have to own up to whatever his role is in all this."

"I guess we'll have to wait and see," Heather said, leaning back against the seat and closing her eyes.

I glanced at the clock, noting that it was nearly five o'clock in the morning. I blew out a sharp breath and took out my phone. I opened a message to Amanda and slowly typed out a long explanation of what had happened, knowing she'd be relieved to know that I was still in one piece and that the danger was over.

"Tell me more about the Rodriguez killing," I asked Kate as she parked outside of the station and shut off the engine.

"Well, it appeared Rodriguez busted the lock between the adjoining rooms. There was a struggle, and Rossi managed to get the upper hand and beat her to death with a table lamp. We found two Glocks and two suppressors in her luggage, so I guess you're right; she was a killer for hire. And it didn't take much digging to connect her with the O'Connor family. In fact, she was rumored to be Patrick O'Connor's girlfriend. The guy Doyle said Rossi killed."

"Who the hell is Patrick O'Connor?" I asked, exasperated, as I followed her into the building, Heather and Samson tagging along behind. "I haven't heard that name before."

"An Irish mob boss," Kate said. "But that's all we have on him."

"Geez," I muttered under my breath as we entered Kate's office. She started a pot of coffee while Heather and I took a seat at the conference table. I figured it would be just fine to let Rossi and Doyle sit and cook for a while.

"Doyle will probably lawyer up," I thought aloud, shaking my head. "I don't think he'll tell us anything, though that conversation he just had with Rossi was a bit of an eye-opener."

"We knew the kid wasn't Rossi's," Heather said, "but never in a million years would I have guessed it was Doyle's. I can't..." She paused and shook her head, then continued, "I can't wrap my head around it. And what's Enzo Massino's involvement? Could it be just Isabella?"

"And Waters," I said. "I'm assuming he worked for Enzo. But who killed him? Rodriguez or Doyle?"

"Who knows?" Heather shook her head and sighed. "But I'm willing to bet it was Doyle, though he'll never admit it."

I watched as Kate poured the three cups of coffee and then handed them round and sat down.

We were all silent, thinking, decompressing.

Me? I hadn't seen any of what had transpired coming, and, honestly, even if I had, it didn't make it any less unbelievable—or confusing. However, the more I thought about it, the kid theory *did* provide plenty of personal motivation for murder. If Doyle was truly insulted about his child being named after Rossi... Well, I've heard more outlandish reasons to commit murder, but to go to the lengths Doyle had... It made no sense.

Could it have made a man like him turn... that murderous? I guess so.

I pondered it as I finished my cup of coffee and then turned to Heather.

"We should call in the rest of the team and wake them up. I need everything they've got on this."

Heather nodded. "I'll give Jacque a call and have her get everyone together. Anything else?"

"Maybe give Isabella Rossi a call?" I suggested. "Maybe tell her that we have her son and that he's facing a murder charge. And maybe throw it out that we know his son isn't his and that it's Doyle's. I think that might get her to start talking—or maybe just knowing that her son is alive and well will do the trick. Either way, if she'll open up, it's going to make this thing a whole lot less confusing."

"Of course," Heather said with a nod. "I'll see what I can do." She looked at her watch. "I guess she might be up and around."

"It doesn't matter. Wake her up," I said. "We need to get to the truth."

"And what about the girlfriend?" Kate threw out. "Shouldn't you be giving her a call, too?"

"Yeah," I said, "that's a good idea. I don't know if I have a number for her. It'd be a hell of a lot easier if we could just bring her in."

"Well, Harry," Heather said, turning to look out the open door. "That *might* just be possible."

I frowned and turned to look. And there she was, the woman we'd been talking about, and she looked angry.

I took a deep breath.

Well now... if that don't beat all.

37

"You found him, then?" Catherine McCarthy raged as she stormed into Kate's office, leaving the uniformed officer standing at the door open-mouthed.

She stalked up to the table and stared down at me, her eyes on fire. She looked like she had been awake for days. Her hair was a mess, and there were dark circles under her eyes.

And I wasn't exactly sure how to take the woman, but I stood up and said, "What are you doing here, Ms. McCarthy?"

"I flew into Atlanta and drove in from there," she huffed. "Now answer my question. Have you found him?"

"Who are you talking about?" I said. "We have Rossi here... and we have Finn Doyle."

"Matty, of course," she said sarcastically, rolling her eyes. "Can I see him?"

"I'll ask again," I said, ignoring her question. "Why are you here in Tennessee?"

"Carmen called Isabella," she said. "I just had to... I had to see him."

I frowned and said, "But he's not the father of your child."

Her eyes went wide. "Um... I..."

"Yes, we know," I told her, "so don't lie to us. We just want to know the truth about what's been going on here."

Catherine glanced past me to Kate and Heather, her lips pursed. "Can I at least sit down and get some coffee? Then... I'll talk?"

"Sure." Kate gestured to a seat at the table opposite her. "Please sit down. How do you take your coffee?"

"Black, please," she replied.

Heather, meanwhile, motioned that she was going to make phone calls. I nodded, and she upped and left without saying a word.

Kate handed Catherine a cup of coffee, which she grabbed with both hands.

"Let's just start all over," I began. "No more garbage. Tell me what's going on with Rossi."

Catherine heaved a sigh, stared down into her cup, and said, "It's all my fault."

I sat back in my chair and folded my arms, unimpressed by the show of emotion.

"Again—" But before I could say more, Kate cut me off.

"Catherine," she said gently. "Just tell us what's going on. Let's start with Rossi. Why did he disappear?"

She lifted her head and looked at Kate. "He and Finn got into an argument, and Matty got angry at him because I was with Finn in one of our off times. Anyway, Finn wasn't around, even though I was madly in love with him. Always it's the bad boys, ya know?"

"No, I don't know," I said, looking at Kate, who was shaking her head at me. "But continue."

"Finn came by one night looking for him—the night before Matty went missing. He said that Matty double-crossed him for Massino and killed one of the O'Connor men. I don't know the specifics. But Finn was out for blood. He said Matty had stolen his son, and now he had gone one step too far. He wanted him dead. The only problem is…"

"Matteo Rossi is really good at disappearing," Kate finished for her. "So he hired Harry."

"Right," Catherine said with a sigh. "I never wanted you to find him, Mr. Starke. I never wanted Finn to find him, either. I just wanted to wash our hands of him and maybe try to be a family, but Isabella… She wanted to find him, too. I just didn't have the heart to tell her, but I think she knew. She's so involved with Massino."

"And you worked for him, Massino, didn't you?" I said, and Kate glared at me.

"Yeah, but it was just a job to get me by," she said. "It wasn't like it meant anything… And Enzo wasn't interested in me. He fired me the first opportunity he had."

I pursed my lips, opting not to press into that subject.

"So Enzo Massino decided to help out Isabella and find Matteo?" Kate said.

"He was supposed to keep him safe." She met my gaze, her eyes dull and sad. "Matteo is a good guy, maybe a little weird. I mean, he just doesn't trust anyone, and once he found out that Matty wasn't his, things shifted. He was there, and Finn wasn't."

"And that's admirable," Kate said.

"Hah, not really," she replied. "Sure, it might look that way, but it was just to get back at Doyle."

"And this O'Connor fellow?" Kate said. "Where does he fit into this?"

"I'm not sure," she answered with a shrug. "I just know that he was an important man, and Matteo was rumored to have whacked him. That's all I know."

"What do you know about Bethany Rodriguez?" Kate asked.

Catherine frowned. "Not much, really. I think she might be

Patrick's girlfriend. I can't really remember all the people that Finn associated with, but I know he was bound and determined that he was going to find Matty."

"Because of Patrick?"

"I guess," Catherine said with a sigh. "I don't know. That's why I'm here. But I was hoping that I could apologize to Matty for this whole mess and let him know I'm changing our son's name."

"I'm sorry," Kate said. "He's in custody. We can't let you see him until he's been interviewed."

Me? I pushed back from the table. I'd had enough of these people, and Catherine McCarthy in particular. She'd shown her true colors, and I wasn't sure I could simply sit and listen to her anymore.

"Take her to the waiting room," Kate said to the uniformed officer, then gave me a look and nodded. I think she could tell I was on the verge of losing my temper. There's nothing worse than being used as a pawn, and that's what Doyle had done. He couldn't find Rossi, so he sent us to do it for him. He wasn't concerned about his *best friend.* He wanted him dead and out of the way.

I gritted my teeth, took a deep breath, pushed past Catherine, and followed Kate to the interrogation rooms. On arrival, she turned to me and said, "Who first? Your choice."

I had no idea who to talk to first. If we chose Doyle, I might be tempted to punch him in the mouth for using me the way he did. Not to mention, what would become of Rossi? Had he killed Rodriguez in self-defense? Probably, but without a witness, I figured it was going to be a hard sell.

Ugh. "Rossi," I said. Kate nodded and opened the door, and I followed her in.

Rossi was seated at the table, his arms folded on the tabletop, staring down at his hands. He'd already been processed, but they hadn't allowed him to wash; he was still covered in blood.

We sat down opposite, and I let Kate take the lead. She read him his rights, then said, "Mr. Rossi. We've just been talking with Catherine McCarthy. She's here in Chattanooga. Did you know that?"

He stared at her, frowned, then shook his head.

"She said your aunt called your mother. Then Catherine came straight here."

He wasn't moved. "So?" he said gloomily.

"We were given to understand the rest of your family has little to do with Carmen," Kate said. "That's not true, is it?"

He shrugged. "My aunt talks to my mother all the time. They set up the car exchange for Nicky. But I'm sure you already figured that out."

I frowned. *Now there's a revelation.*

"I thought it was something like that," Kate said. "And they did that to help you?"

Again, he shrugged, then looked down at the table and said, "Nick was supposed to meet me at the hotel. I was supposed to meet him in the parking lot at ten, but when I walked out, I saw Doyle standing at his window. I don't know how he found him. But then, I don't know how Doyle does a lot of the things he does. I thought he and I were friends. Just shows how wrong you can be, right?"

"And then what happened?" I asked.

He looked at me without speaking for a moment, then said, "He shot him, and I got out of there, didn't I?"

"Tell us about Patrick O'Connor," I said. "Doyle said you killed him."

He nodded. "It was self-defense. Patrick was Finn's buddy. He invited me out for a couple of drinks. I thought I might be getting a promotion. I've been a mule for them for years, and I thought I might be moving up, you know?" He looked at me as if waiting for some kind of confirmation, then when he didn't get one, he continued, "but that's not what happened. Patrick drew on me. He was going to kill me…" He trailed off.

"And?" I said.

"And I was faster than him, Mr. Starke." Rossi met my gaze. "It was just that simple. I've always been quick. We were at a bar. He told me he needed to talk to me, private like. So I followed him outside. There was something about his attitude I didn't get, so I was antsy, like, you know? He was just ahead of me. He made some sort of smart remark. I saw him put his hand under his jacket, and he stopped and turned, pulling his gun. As I said, I was quicker than him." He shrugged. "After that, I knew I had to go. I couldn't hang around or I was gonna end up getting my whole family killed, and I cared about the kid and Catherine, too. She kept going with Finn, but she kept coming back, and I kept letting her."

"So Doyle wanted to get rid of you because she came back to you?" Kate asked, frowning.

"Yup, that's about the size of it. Once he makes up his mind to do something, he's relentless. I knew he was going to eliminate me however he could. I knew I was up against a whole army of people, and I was hoping like hell you weren't one of them, Mr. Starke. Am I going to prison?"

I looked at Kate.

"You'll be held while we continue our investigation. What happens after that depends on the outcome. You're probably going to go on trial for your crimes, and all I can tell you is that you need a damn good lawyer. You're going to be fighting an uphill battle, I'm afraid." She looked at me, her eyebrows raised in question.

"I would imagine Enzo Massino can help you out with that,"

I said, "if he doesn't hold the murder of Nick Waters over your head."

"Nah, Ma won't let him. She's got that man wrapped around her finger. It's good for her. I just wish she'd have stayed out of this. It's my mess. She shoulda let me deal with it."

"You'd probably be dead by now," I said.

"Maybe." He leaned back in the chair. "But at least she wouldn't be under the microscope. I don't want her getting into any trouble."

"What about Bethany Rodriguez?" Kate asked. "What happened?"

He raised his eyebrows, sucked on his bottom lip, thinking, then said, "Beth was... She was Pat's girlfriend. I didn't know she was in the room next to me. I couldn't sleep. I heard some clicking on the adjoining door. I didn't know what it was, but I figured it was something. So I got up out of bed, grabbed the lamp and stood behind the door. She came in. I knocked the gun out of her hand with the lamp and... I hit her... and I hit her again... and again..." He trailed off and shrugged. "She would have killed me."

He looked traumatized, numb, and I couldn't help but feel a pang of sympathy, however brief.

Well, at least he's still alive. Isabella could be charged with aiding and abetting, I suppose... if they have the energy to pursue it. Hah, we'll be lucky to figure this debacle of a case out.

I looked at Kate. She nodded, then looked at Rossi and said, "You want to talk to Catherine? She's here."

He frowned, then said, "I think I'll pass."

"Good choice," I said. "You're already in enough trouble."

38

"Let's have a word with Finn Doyle," I said as Kate closed the door to Rossi's room.

She nodded. Doyle's room was next door to Rossi's. She opened the door, and we stepped inside.

Doyle was seated in much the same position as Rossi, except he had his arms folded and a confident smirk on his face. Everything about him set me on edge and made me want to knock the smirk right off his face. But I kept my cool and pulled out a chair, as did Kate.

"Ah, there you are, then, the two of you. I was wonderin' if they'd let you talk to me, Mr. Starke. After all, you're not a cop, now are ya?"

Kate read him his rights, then looked at me. But before I could speak, Doyle started talking.

"If you're thinking oi manipulated you, Mr. Starke, you'd be incorrect."

"How so?" I said, caustically, and leaned back and folded my arms. My head was still aching from the blows I'd received at the hands of Bethany Rodriguez, and so was my back, so I was in no mood for idle chitchat with the glib Irishman.

"Well, for starters," Doyle said, his chin down almost to his chest, "Rossi and I were good friends, so we were. We were close. I got to know his family very well. But I wasn't doing it for the right reasons. Y'see, I had me eye on his girlfriend, Catherine. She's a looker, and way out of his league, if y'get me drift."

Here we go, I thought.

"So I started seeing her on the side, and she got kinda stuck between the two of us. She thought Rossi was a good man and didn't deserve what she was doing to him, but me? I thought he was a bit of an annoyance, don't y'see? And all I wanted to do was take care of the problem. Now, she didn't like that idea at all, and she broke t'ings off with me entirely about four months into her pregnancy."

I *really* didn't care about the domestic timeline, and the more I listened, the more annoyed I became.

"So, you decided to have your friend Patrick take him out?" I said.

Doyle narrowed his eyes. "I did nut'in' of the sort." He sounded genuinely offended. "But now y'mention it, I t'ink I want me lawyer… now."

"Of course. Then we're done here?" Kate said.

"It was a pleasure, Captain, Mr. Starke. And you." He looked at me. "You have no idea how helpful you were. You were connecting the dots for me all along. And you beat me at my own game, so y'did. Impressive."

"I'll have Jacque send you a refund," I said.

Doyle laughed. "No need. You did your job. You found Rossi."

I shook my head. "No, thanks. I don't want your dirty money. Have a good life, what's left of it. Let's go, Kate," and we did.

I stepped to the door, grabbed the handle, opened it and stood aside for Kate.

"All done?" a voice in the hallway said.

I looked out to see two men in blue suits, along with the desk sergeant, standing there, smiling. *Feds*, I thought to myself. *That was quick.*

"He's asked for a lawyer," Kate said. "Good luck. He's a total ass."

"Nothing we're not used to," the shorter one said as he stepped past me into the room.

"Mr. Doyle, I'm—"

The rest I didn't hear as his partner closed the door, still smiling.

∽

KATE AND I SPLIT: she to the break room and me to the parking lot where I met Heather, who was waiting for Jacque to come pick us up. She was standing on the front steps, nursing a mug of coffee.

"Hey," she said. "How'd it go?"

"About as I expected," I replied. "Rossi loosened up a little, and Doyle lawyered up."

"Yeah," she said. "I was in the observation room. I listened. Crazy how it all came down to a dispute over a woman." Heather laughed, shaking her head.

"Not as crazy as you might think," I replied. "Women have been the cause of many a war going all the way back into prehistory. Remember Helen of Troy?"

She smiled.

I nodded to a couple more feds as they passed by.

"I called Isabella Rossi," she said.

"Oh, yes? How did that go?"

"First, she cried with relief. Then she admitted she set it up for Waters to take Carmen's car. Other than that... she seemed okay. I don't think she had anything to do with... anything else connected to this mess. She seemed stressed, for sure, but I think that was because she wants to get Matteo a proper lawyer."

"Yes," I said. "He's going to need one."

I rubbed my forehead. I was just about overcome with fatigue, and I was hurting all over. Even so, I figured it was a good night to be up.

It was already getting light. I looked at my watch. It was just after six. I shook my head. It had been a long day and night.

"You think Matteo Rossi is a bad guy?" Heather asked, then sipped her coffee.

"I don't know. I suppose that's for a jury to decide. I think he's a complex character, and obviously dangerous. He readily admitted to killing two people, and I wouldn't be surprised if there were more, given his job."

"Yeah, I suppose you're right."

"But you know what?" I said.

"What's that, Harry?" Heather chuckled as she gazed up at me.

"I think it's time for us to let the professionals handle this. I don't know about you, but I'm ready to get out of here and get some sleep. We did all we can, and the feds, being the feds, won't want anything more from us other than our files."

"You're not wrong about that," Heather agreed, looking at her watch. "Jacque's on her way. I'd drive you home myself, but my car's in the impound lot."

I nodded, then said, "That was a fine piece of driving you did."

"Yes, well, not fine enough, I think. Geez, I'm glad this one is over."

"Yes," I said. "Me, too."

Two more feds ran by into the building, their jackets flapping open, and I thought about Kate having to deal with the annoying men in blue suits. *Rather her than me,* I thought, then smiled to myself. *That's why she's a captain, and I'm not.*

I was always one to blur the lines to get to the truth, but thankfully, with this case, I didn't have to do that. Though I had to admit that my client, the inimitable Finn Doyle, was a thoroughly bad guy.

"We've got to get that refund check sent soon. I don't want the man's money," I muttered, more to myself than to Heather.

"Jacque's already taken care of it," Heather said and patted my arm.

I looked up at the awakening sky. It was an azure field dotted with fluffy white clouds. The breath of fresh morning air was just the tonic I needed. It was going to be a beautiful day.

A few moments later, Jacque pulled up in front of us, rolled down the window, and said, "All right, kids, time to go." Her eyebrows were up, and she gifted us with what I can only describe as a quizzical smile. I could only imagine what we must have looked like: ragged and worn from the crash, the car chase, and a day and a half fraught with danger.

"I'm going to be sore tomorrow," Heather mumbled as she climbed into the back seat. "And it's going to be a whole lot of fun trying to explain this one to my insurance agent."

"I'm sure they've heard it all," I said as I gently eased my aching body into the passenger seat and reached for my seat belt.

"So, we're in the hole on this one," Jacque said as she pulled out onto Amnicola. "You know it's a total loss once we issue that refund."

"I'll take the loss, Jacque. You know it's the right thing to do."

"I can't argue with you on that, but that doesn't change the facts," she grumbled. "But you know, I never pegged Finn Doyle as the scorned and jealous lover."

"I think we should stop by McDonald's," I said. "I could go for a sausage biscuit and a cup of coffee."

"Sounds like you're feeling better, Harry." Jacque chuckled. "Maybe it wasn't just the stomach bug that was getting to you."

"And maybe my gut was in overdrive," I thought aloud.

I leaned back and closed my eyes. "I have to admit, I didn't see any of this coming," I said.

"I did," Jacque quipped. "The moment I laid eyes on the photo of that kid, I knew there was something amiss. Love and greed are strong motives."

"I really don't feel like sitting through one of your lessons right now, Jacque," Heather griped from the back seat. "I just want an egg McMuffin and maybe a couple of Ibuprofen. I think I'm already feeling the results of that fender bender."

I turned, looked at her and smiled.

"Me, too," I said. "Me, too. We got lucky, Heather, thanks to you."

39

One month later...

"Have you read these articles?" Amanda slid the morning newspaper across the table to me. "It's amazing the stories they've put out about Doyle."

"It's sensationalized," I said as I picked up my cup of coffee.

"But I can't believe he consented to all these interviews," Amanda continued. "And he never did cash the refund, did he?"

"I don't want to talk about it," I said and rustled the newspaper to emphasize the point.

"You're still mad about it, aren't you?" Amanda giggled at the pounding of little feet running into the kitchen. "Good morning, Jade," she said and leaned over and gave our daughter a kiss on the top of her head.

"Good morning, Momma," Jade said, beaming.

I gave my daughter a smile. "Hey, sweetie," I said and scooted my chair back far enough for her to crawl up into my lap. "What're we going to do today?"

"Momma promised me she would make me pancakes." Jade

tilted her head and looked at Amanda, her little eyebrows raised. Amanda reached out and squeezed her hand.

"Of course, I will. Why don't you go get dressed? You can wear whatever you like today."

"Ooh!" Jade squealed, squirmed off my lap and took off running back to her room.

"It's amazing the little things that make her happy," I said, took another sip of my coffee and picked up the paper. "I wish everyone was just as content as she is."

"Me, too," Amanda said, pushing back from the table. "But I guess if life was really that easy, then you wouldn't have a job, would you?"

"Touché." I laughed and glanced down at the paper, taking in the picture of Doyle front and center, that same irritating smirk plastered across his face. There was something about the man that ground on my nerves. Was it the fact that the son of a bitch had refused to take the refund?

I *really* didn't want his money, but what bothered me even more was my concern that he was somehow planning to use it against me. It wouldn't have been the first time a mobster had done such a thing. I scanned the article, rolling my eyes at the way he'd managed to glorify himself.

"This isn't good," I muttered, shaking my head. "I just don't understand the public's fascination with a mobster."

"You'd be an anomaly, I'm afraid," Amanda commented as she took a mixing bowl from the cupboard. "For as long as organized crime has been around, it's fascinated people. They're always going to find something interesting about it. Look at Al Capone, John Gotti and that rat Sammy 'The Bull' Gravano. Now there's a character for you. An admitted killer and utterly fearless."

"Yeaah, I get it, but you know what I find interesting?" I set my mug down and looked up at her.

"What's that?" she asked, not looking back at me as she grabbed the packet of premade pancake mix.

"Doyle's crime wasn't mob related. He did what he did because he was jealous."

"And Catherine McCarthy is going to be lucky if she gets off with just a slap on the wrist," Amanda said, measuring out the pancake mix and then dumping it into the mixing bowl. "So many people knew what was going on, and no one did anything about it."

"That's typical," I said, folding up the newspaper.

"And in those articles, it doesn't mention a *thing* about Rossi," she said. "He's still a faceless man. Don't you find that fascinating?"

"Not anymore," I said. "The kid has a rap sheet now, a mug shot and the beginnings of a digital footprint. And the government he feared so much now has him firmly in its grasp. Kind of ironic, don't you think?"

"Yes," she replied. "Did you ever learn if his suspicions that his father was killed by the government rather than just having a heart attack were true?"

"No, we didn't. Isabella Rossi insisted it was a heart attack, and nobody ever provided anything to counter that."

I leaned back in my chair and watched as she stirred the mixture. "I still have to wonder, though, what's going to happen to the guy. I have to admit, I can't help but feel a little sad about the situation."

"Why's that?" she asked. "Because his son wasn't actually his?"

"No, well, I mean, *yes,*" I answered. "That is sad, but also, I think the man might've done better for himself. He didn't have to go to work for Doyle, but he did; he chose a life of crime. Everyone said how nice he was as a kid. He could've had a life. Now, he's probably going to jail for a long time."

"Maybe," Amanda reasoned. "He'll go on trial. He has a good case for self-defense in both deaths. He may well be acquitted. He's got a good lawyer. One of the best criminal defense attorneys in New York City."

"Thanks to yet another mafia don." I took a deep breath. "But really, why won't Doyle take the refund? I just know he's playing some kind of game."

"Why don't you get rid of it, Harry?" Amanda said, turning her head to look at me. "Give it to a charity that could do some good with it."

"Hmm," I said, thinking about the idea. "You might have something there."

"Turn what Doyle meant for bad into something good."

"Any ideas what kind of charity?" I said.

"How about an organization that's trying to help kids stay on the right path? Keep them away from getting into a life of crime to begin with," Amanda said, grabbing the whisk.

"Good idea," I agreed. "Maybe the money can help some other kids stay out of the kind of trouble Rossi got into."

She set the bowl down on the counter, grabbed a pan, and turned on the stove in the process. "Any charities come to mind?" she said, smiling.

I scrunched up my eyes, thinking about the charities I knew of in Chattanooga. "A few. And you?" She had a familiar twinkle in her eye, the one that told me she already had an answer.

She placed her finger in the dimple on her chin, pretending like she was giving it solid thought. "I would give it to the non-profit the Chattanooga Police Department works with. You know, the one that helps keep the kids off the streets and gives them alternatives if they've started getting into trouble."

My jaw dropped. "That's perfect."

"Besides, if Doyle finds out, he'll be extremely irritated." Amanda shot me a playful wink. And I laughed.

She nodded her head toward the pancake mix. "You want to help me with these?"

Thank you for reading *Duplicity* the twenty-third book in the Harry Starke Novels. I hope you enjoyed it, if you did please help others find Blair Howards Books by leaving a few words about it in the form of a review.

HARRY STARKE WILL BE BACK WITH HIS NEXT CASE SOON!

DON'T MISS THIS

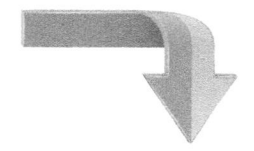

SIGN UP FOR ANNOUNCEMENTS & GREAT DEALS!
PLUS you'll Unlock 20% Off
Get Exclusive Deals (As Part Of "The Family")
Visit www.BlairHowardBooks.com
If you don't see the pop up to join, just click the blue unlock 20% off icon and enter your details.
Don't forget to confirm your email and whitelist (save as contact)Blair@blairhowardbooks.com to your email system.

From Blair Howard

The Harry Starke Genesis Series
The Harry Starke Series
The Lt. Kate Gazzara Murder Files
Randall & Carver Mysteries
The Peacemaker Series
The Civil War Series

From Blair C. Howard

The Sovereign Star Series

ABOUT THE AUTHOR

Blair Howard is a retired journalist turned novelist. He's the author of more than 50 novels including the international bestselling Harry Starke series of crime stories, the Lt. Kate Gazzara series, and the Harry Starke Genesis series. He's also the author of the Peacemaker series of international spy thrillers and five Civil War/Western novels.

If you enjoy reading Science Fiction thrillers, Mr. Howard has made his debut into the genre with, The Sovereign Stars Series under the name, Blair C. Howard.

Visit www.blairhowardbooks.com.

You can also find Blair Howard on Social Media

Copyright © 2024 Duplicity by Blair Howard
The Harry Starke Novels Book 23

All rights reserved.
Printed 2024 Cleveland, TN
Print ISBN: 979-8-9908529-0-7
Library of Congress Control Number: Pending
Email: BlairHoward@BlairHowardBooks.com
www.blairhowardbooks.com

No part of this publication may be reproduced, stored in a retrieval system, or transmitted in any form, or by any means, electronic, mechanical, photocopying, recording, or otherwise, without the express written permission of the publisher except for the use of brief quotations in a book review.

This book is protected under the copyright laws of the United States of America. Any reproduction or other unauthorized use of the material or artwork herein is prohibited.

Disclaimer: Duplicity is a work of fiction, the product of the author's imagination. The persons and events depicted in this novel were also created by the author's imagination; no resemblance to actual persons or events is intended.

Made in the USA
Monee, IL
04 May 2025